Scorched

A Dry Earth Novel, Volume 1

Theresa Shaver

This is a work of fiction. Similarities to real people, places, or events are entirely coincidental.

SCORCHED

First edition. Print. September 18, 2017.

Copyright © 2017 Theresa Shaver.

ISBN: 978-0-9959381-2-0

Written by Theresa Shaver.

Cover Art by Melchelle Designs

Author's Note

This book is NOT the third book in the Endless Winter Series you have been waiting for. I'm sorry! Sun & Smoke was meant to come next but this little adventure novel kicked it out of my head and wouldn't stop until the last word was written. I hope the fast pace and flow comes through as the book is set over a few days. This book contains no swear words and only the thinnest reference to sex. So I would gauge the reading age to be 13+. This book is not as dark as my previous books but still a fun read set in a wrecked world. I would like to set another book, down the line in this world but not until the other two series are complete. I hope you enjoy my very first standalone novel and as always, thank you so much for sticking with me on this amazing writing journey! Please review to let me know what you think.

Xoxo

Theresa

A couple of points about some of the tech in the book:

Hover sleds: are a Back to the Future kind of thing so it was a surprise to find out in my research that they already exist and are being used in some heavy industries. I'm eagerly awaiting the day I can go buy one at Home Depot!

Dune buggies: Solar power dune buggies are all the rage on the desert racing circuit…who knew!

Hand rail cart: We've all see the cartoons with two tired guys pumping away at the handle on a rail cart. When researching them for dimensions I found that they were heavily used in Japan as people transports in the early 1900's and they were fully enclosed with seats as seen in the image below. I made mine slightly larger.

The image below was taken from Wikipedia showing Matsuyama Handcar Tramway at Osaki City Matsuyama Furusato History Museum.

Chapter One

I huff out a breath of despair as the thin trickle of water dribbles out of the hand pump. I close my eyes and pump harder as I pray for the sound of gushing, but it doesn't come. The bucket is only half filled by the time my arm gives out from the pumping. There's no fixing it so I drop to my butt onto the dry, cracked ground sending a puff of dust wafting up around me and lean back against the cool metal pipe that will be scorching hot in a few hours once the sun rises above the house. Tilting my head back, I scan the sky for clouds that might bring the desperately needed rain, but just like most days of my life there are none to be found. These few minutes, first thing in the morning, is the only time during the day that being outside is tolerable. I close my eyes and let thoughts of a better life, a better world, consume me.

The slap of the old, wooden screen door hitting the frame brings me right back to the bleak reality of my life as my little sister comes barreling towards me.

"Día! Abuela says to hurry up. She's going to make breakfast!"

This has me surging to my feet in concern. Grandmother hasn't left her bed in weeks. Every morning, I peek into her room and expect her to have passed away in the night. Her being up either means she's recovered or it's the final spurt of her long life.

I study my small sister and bite my lip. She's so delicate, I don't know how she will survive Abuela's passing. Everything about my sister worries me. She's so small for her age. Nine years old and she could pass for a six-year-old. Stunted growth from not enough food and water her whole life. The delicate bones in her face and wrists make me think of glass that can be shattered at any moment. The only thing healthy about my sister is her attitude. I swear, she shines brighter than the sun that is slowly killing us all. It makes her nickname fitting when I shorten her name to Glo.

"DÍA! Are you even listening to me? She's up, up, UP!"

My lips can't resist the tug of a smile that pulls on them as she does a bopping dance around me.

"Ok, ok … let's go see what she's cooking up." I laugh as she dashes for the back door.

I grab the partially-filled bucket and follow at a slower pace, half thrilled Abuela is moving around and half wary of what it means. I catch the screen door before it can smack against the frame and see that the top hinge is almost completely out of the rotting wood again. Just one more thing that's falling apart. I stand just inside the kitchen and observe the woman who has basically raised us since my mother took off eight years ago.

She's a head shorter than me, maybe even more now that her back has curved with age. Hair the color of steel is tied tightly at the nape of her neck but it still sways across her slim back as she moves from cupboard to cupboard inventorying what's left of our food. It's been weeks since she's been in this kitchen so it's a lot emptier than the last time she was here. I take a step into the room, causing her head to whip my way. I catch the quick glimpse of fear in her watered-down indigo eyes before she can mask it. All I can do is nod my head at her. Yes, it is as grim as it looks.

She turns away as I step up beside her and place the water bucket onto the counter.

"Abuela, it's good to have you here. This room misses you." I whisper as I lean over and plant a kiss on her head.

Her hand reaches out and grasps my wrist tightly before it turns into a pat on the arm.

She sniffs. "Well, I might be old but I'm not dead yet, girlie! Figured I should get these old bones moving while I still can." She ends on a laugh but we both know her time is drawing near.

She rises up on her toes and peers down into the bucket before settling back onto her feet with a sigh. "The well?"

I take a quick glance over my shoulder but see that Gloria is occupied, humming to herself as she plays with her rag dolls in the corner so I turn back and shake my head.

"Almost played out. That was an hour of pumping."

Her shoulders slump but then firm up and she turns hard eyes on me. "Time to make some plans then. But first, breakfast!"

I nod and step back, relief flooding through me. I have no idea what to do next, hopefully she does. I busy myself with transferring a quarter of the water from the bucket into our old watering can. I try not to wince when I see Abuela dump the last few cups of our flour into a mixing bowl. I have no idea where I will get more so I turn away, hoping she knows what she's doing and I leave the room with the watering can.

I head into the small glass atrium my grandfather built onto the side of the house decades ago for his beloved wife to grow her roses. It's been many years since anyone in this house has had the luxury of growing anything but food in this room. All the lower windows have been papered over to keep prying eyes off of our life support crops. People will kill for what we have now. It also helps keep the scorching sun from withering the plants to dust. The ceiling glass panes are crisscrossed with duct tape where they have cracked over the years and we have a fabric curtain on levers to close off the worst of the midday sun. I go about the many tiers, dribbling out the water that will keep the plants growing and us alive. The watering can has barely an inch of water left when I get to the end of the row where my favorite pots are. Two stunted trees stand in the corner. One with oranges and one with limes. They yield less and less fruit every year but they are my favorites all the same. I split the water between the two and gently pull one of each fruit from each tree and head back into the kitchen. I need to eat and then get back to pumping the well. Half of a bucket won't be enough for the three of us for the day.

The table is set for three and Gloria has added a few of her precious fake flowers as a centerpiece. She's treating the meal as a celebration because grandma is up with us. I think it might be the last good meal we have. I slice the fruit and divide it evenly on our three plates. It seems like such a pitiful amount. Abuela carries a small platter to the table with a stack of freshly made tortillas next to a mound of scrambled eggs with red and green peppers mixed in. My mouth starts watering even though I know the eggs come from a powder and will have the texture of sand. I lift my gaze from the biggest meal we've had in weeks and meet her eyes. They almost dare me to object to the amount of food she's made but I don't. Instead, I send her the biggest smile I can muster with all the love and gratitude I feel for her in my eyes. Her expression softens and with a nod, she settles between me and Gloria as we bow our heads to pray. I sit quietly waiting while they list their thanks but don't contribute. I'm pretty sure He stopped listening a long time ago.

Gloria chatters her way through the meal but I'm distracted by all the things I have to do today and what we will eat tomorrow now that Abuela has nearly wiped out our basics with this one meal. I'm so lost in thought that it takes her a few times saying my name for me to notice.

"Claudia! I know I'm an excellent cook but try to focus on something other than the food!" She teases.

I smile. "Sorry, I was just planning my day."

Abuela makes a "tsk" sound with her tongue at me. "Such a young girl to have so many responsibilities on her shoulders. Even during the hardest times, you must learn to enjoy the small moments of life that will bring us happiness if we allow it."

I nod my head in agreement. "Of course. What were you saying?"

She studies me with her penetrating eyes for a moment before glancing down at her plate.

"After we clean up breakfast, we must prepare to go to the ration station."

My eyes widen in disbelief. How can she even suggest such a thing when it was her that determined months ago that it was too dangerous to continue going to the station? I look over at Gloria and see her practically bouncing in her seat with excitement. None of us have left the house except for the yard since the last time we went to the station.

I heave out a breath and push away my plate. "We can't do that! The last time we went we only made it home with half the rations we got and you almost broke your hip! Things will have gotten even worse there by now!"

She sends me a glare with a slight tilt of her head at Gloria causing me to flash a worried look her way. We had made up a story of tripping on the rough road to explain away our injuries to her instead of the truth. I can still picture the mob of people desperate for food and water pushing and shoving when the trucks ran out of supplies.

"Día, I understand your fears but we must get some supplies for what's ahead."

I open my mouth to object but then slam it shut at the look in her eyes. She talking about when she's gone. She must feel her time is coming. She wants to do this now so I don't have to face it alone. Once again, I bow my head. This time I do pray and it's to get us all through this day safely.

After we use a tiny amount of the water to clean the dishes, we gather the two rickety wagons we have and I fill them with empty jugs that will hopefully be filled with clean water at the station. I go searching for the gear we will need for being outside most of the day. The three battered umbrellas we will need to protect us from the sun while standing in the long lines, scarves to cover our heads and goggles for if the wind whips up the dust. Gloria is vibrating with excitement as she and I stand waiting by the front door for Abuela.

"I can't WAIT to see Maria! It's been so long. We have so much to catch up on!"

I stifle a laugh. How much can there be for a nine-year-old to catch up on when she never leaves the house? I shoot her a wink anyway. I'm glad we can give her this small excitement. Maria's family lives two blocks from the station and they have always been happy to have Glo stay with them while we go stand in line. It's not safe for such a small girl to go with us. It also gives her a chance to be around other children. Something I know she desperately needs.

"Only one wagon, child, and no jugs."

I turn confused as Abuela comes down the hallway towards us. She has a faded scarf covering her hair and a messenger bag slung across her chest. I can give her many reasons why we need both wagons and the jugs to make this worth doing but instead just shake my head and ask, "Why?"

"We will only be doing the ration station today and I'm sure they won't be giving out enough to fill two wagons! Now, do you have our ration cards? We will need all three to get the most supplies we can."

I nod my head that I have them but continue staring at her, waiting for her to explain. She's stubborn, just like me so it goes on for a few minutes until my patience runs out. I finally just throw up my hands and say, "The well?"

She crosses her arms and gives me her best 'don't mess with me' look. "Never mind the well! Do as I say, girl."

When I don't move, just return her stare, she finally gives in. "Día, I am an old woman with many years behind me. I ask that you trust that I know what I'm doing. We will go to the station and get the rations as fast as we can. Once we are back, I will explain what we will do from there. Now, vamos!"

I sigh deeply but turn to the door. I'm now starting to worry that with age, her mind might be slipping too.

Chapter Two

The wagon is light without all the jugs we would have needed so it only takes a few minutes to get it down the front stairs to the street. The three of us move quickly down the lane past the few deserted homes that are left standing. Once we reach the intersection, we turn left towards the main part of town. It's an easy twenty-minute walk to the station but every moment that slips by, the sun is rising in the sky ratcheting up the temperature. I don't look to the sides where empty homes sit, some burnt down, some falling down - but most are just empty.

When I was younger than Glo, there were more people that lived here. Now it just feels like a shell of a town. Abuela says that the climate here has always been hot but livable when there was something called air-conditioning. When the sun started its temper tantrum, as she calls it, and made the whole world hotter, people fled to the north where the temperatures were more manageable. She says that's where Mama went, but with the wall they built to keep out the refugees, I don't know why she bothered. I can only be grateful that it isn't summer or we would be going to the station in the dark. The temperatures we have now in the winter months are what the summer months used to be. Summer temperatures now are unbearable during the daylight hours and we can only be outside at night. We sleep during the day down in our basement where it's a few degrees cooler. I hate those four months of the year.

We reach the street that Maria and her family live on and turn onto it. There is more life here, more people. Many families moved into the abandoned houses closer to the stations so they wouldn't have as far to walk to get the meager supplies and water the government still hands out. There are a few kids playing in the dry dirt in front of a house halfway down the street. One of them pops to her feet and barrels toward us.

"Glo, Glo, GLO!" She shouts with childish glee before crashing into my small sister. Thin arms with sharp elbows wrap around each other as they dance in place.

"Maria Elena! You will break that child in two!"

I pull my eyes from my sister's beaming face to see Maria's mother standing on the stoop.

"Silvia! How are you?" Abuela calls out as we walk towards her.

Silvia takes in the wagon I'm pulling and frowns. "Bonita, it's good to see you out and about. It's been months, I was worried about you."

My grandmother laughs. "You are too kind. We are just fine but hoping we can impose on you."

Silvia waves her words away. "It's never an imposition to have Gloria here. She will occupy these monsters for a few hours and keep them out of my hair!" She glances at the wagon again and bites her lip.

"You are going to the station, yes?" When we nod, she shoos the children away to the back yard. Gloria runs with them without a backward glance at us.

"There are armed guards there now to keep control but once out of the square, there are animals just waiting to take people's rations from them. You must be very careful once you leave the square. Two women alone would make a tempting target for them. I wish I could send Juan with you but he's found some work and won't be back until after sunset."

Abuela keeps a smile on her face as she nods in understanding. "We will be just fine, Silvia. Thank you for watching Gloria and for the warning."

Silvia opens her mouth to say more but changes her mind and just nods in understanding. She knows that everything is a risk now and we all must take them to keep living.

I glance back when we get to the end of her street and see that she is still watching us so I raise my hand in a short wave before turning the corner. If this day goes bad, at least Gloria will be with good people who will watch over her.

The closer we get to the main square where the stations are the more nervous I become. The last time we were here the noise was overwhelming. People were yelling, screaming and crying as the mob took control. Now I hear nothing and the silence feels ominous to me. I glance over at Abuela but she has a determined expression that she's fixed firmly ahead. The way she keeps clutching and releasing the strap of her bag tells me she's just as nervous as I am.

The first block we pass, we don't see anyone except a few curtains shifting as people look out. It's the second block that has me tensing up. We've moved from residential to the commercial area and there are men lounging in doorways and on steps. They watch us go by like a hawk watches his prey. They know we have nothing of value they want yet but the return trip with the rations will be a different story.

We've almost reached the square when a voice rings out that has me gritting my teeth and clenching my fists.

"Hey, Indigo? Where have you been hiding? I miss seeing those eyes, Chica!"

As my grandmother and I share the same distinct eye color, we both turn our heads to the voice. Neither of us happy to hear it.

Sitting on the stoop of an abandoned flower shop, surrounded by men, is one of the worst people this town has to offer - Boyd Baker. Before school was shut down seven years ago, I was in the same grade as his younger brother, Beckam. We were friends for a few years. I liked how quiet he was and how he loved to read as much as I did. That all came to stop one day when his big brother was bullying him and I tried to intervene. All I got for my efforts was some scrapes and bruises when Boyd shoved me to the ground and Beck never speaking to me again.

We turned our heads away from the group and kept on walking. But my feet slam to a stop when Boyd yells out, "We'll see if you want to talk when you head back this way with something more interesting!"

I turn my body slowly until I'm facing him and tilt my head slightly to the side while meeting his smirking eyes.

"Does that mean you're going to attack us? Steal the little bit of food an old lady and two young girls need to live on?" I keep my tone even - like I'm really curious to know if that's his plan. When I see the smirk slowly leave his face, I hit him with a parting shot. "Cause if that's what's in store for us, I can just bring Gloria over right now for you to kill. It would be much faster that way."

I don't show the satisfaction I feel when he looks away with a wave of his hand for us to carry on. Inside though, I'm happy my words hit the mark. I've known from an early age that facing a bully down is always better than waiting for them to strike. Abuela pulls at my arm to get me moving again but doesn't speak until we are almost at the end of the block.

"Día, you make me so proud and terrified all at the same time! That was a huge risk you just took."

I drape my arm around her shoulders as we enter the square. "Just breathing is a risk these days."

The sight that greets us in the square is so far from what was here the last time. Two lines of beaten down people on opposite sides of the square await us. No one is speaking and all eyes are cast down to the dusty stones. It's not hard to see why, with the soldiers standing guard along each line with huge guns. I'm distracted by the sight of them so I don't see what's right in front of us and almost trip when Abuela comes to an abrupt stop.

"State your business here!" A deep voice barks.

There's a pair of soldiers blocking our way. I'm so startled that instinctively I look behind me for a place to run. That's why I see Boyd's group of men pull a guy carrying a ration box and a jug of water into the closest alleyway. I guess *his* family won't be eating tonight.

"Día! Show these nice men our ration cards so we can line up!"

I turn my head back around and fumble for the cards in my front pocket. My hand only trembles slightly when I hand them over. One of them snatches the cards from my hand and scans them before hitting me with a piercing glare.

"Why do you have three? Did you steal one of these?"

I'm shaking my head in denial but Abuela is already speaking in soothing tones to him.

"No, no, my small granddaughter. She is too little to stand in the sun all day. I didn't feel it was safe for her to come. See, see on the card? She is just a small girl."

He stares her down but she just gives a pleasant smile back so he finally shrugs and hands all the cards back to me and motions with his gun for us to enter the square. I let out a breath I didn't even know I was holding in as we rush past them and join the ration line on the west side of the square.

Once we are in place, I take a better look around at both lines. It's a sad sight. There are less than half of the people that were here the last time and the ones that are left look more like the old-world make-believe zombies than real people. Everyone shuffles forward as the lines move but no one makes eye contact or speaks to anyone else. I take a closer look at the soldiers but they all look relaxed and bored. There's not much else to do or see so I just zone out and make a list in my head of all the things I need to get done back at the house.

We shuffle along with everyone else but I'm pleased to see we are close to the front of the line after only an hour and a half. That's less than half the time it used to take. I've still sweated through most of my shirt but I'm grateful there was no wind today to pelt us with dust. Abuela says we are acclimatized to the heat from being born into it but I don't feel like I'm used to it. When we reach the table, an impatient man barely looks at us as he swipes the ration cards from my hand. Once he has swiped them in his fancy machine though, he pauses and looks closer at it before giving us a better look over.

"You haven't gotten rations for over thirty days? It says you're due quite a lot here! I can't give all that to you today!"

Abuela gives him a reassuring smile. "No, no señor, of course not! We would be most grateful for anything you can spare for us today."

He looks at her and then me for a moment before his shoulders slump.

"You also have a child at home to feed?" At our nods, he looks back at the line behind us and then at the soldiers. "Ok, give me your wagon. Push it under the table…discreetly!"

I'm confused but I do as he says. We wait as he pulls it with him behind a temporary screen barrier. Usually, they just hand us our three small boxes and we walk away so this is very strange. I glance at Abuela with a raised eyebrow but she gives a tiny shake of her head so I stay silent.

When he returns, I catch a glimpse of the wagon but its bed is covered with some kind of burlap sack so I can't see what's inside of it. He pushes it back under the table towards us but then also hands us the standard ration boxes from under his arm. As Abuela reaches for hers, he leans in towards her and whispers urgently.

"You must make this last!" He glances around again. "Do you understand?" Her eyes go wide but she gives him a slow, grim nod so he releases the box to her but speaks again. "Wait for a bigger group to leave the square first then follow them. Do you understand?" Again, she nods her head so he pulls back with a muttered, "Good luck."

We turn away from the table and he waits until we've moved five feet away before calling for the next in line. It's then that I remember he didn't return our ration cards so I turn to go back but Abuela's hand snakes out and stops me with a painful grip on my wrist.

"Our cards…" I say but she cuts me off.

"Leave them, they are useless to us now."

I want to argue but she pulls me further away from the table to the middle of the square.

"Día, you need to trust me and keep your questions until we get home!" When I nod my head with confusion, she releases my wrist and pats my arm. "Now, which way shall we go? Back towards the devil we know or face the unknown?"

I scan the four exits to the square but they all look the same to me. She's asking if we should chance Boyd's group and hope they don't rob us or go a different way. I'm guessing that there are predators waiting at every exit but right now there is a group of six heading out of the square where we came in, so safety in numbers might be the best way to go. I point that way and lift the wagon handle to get it moving. It's much heavier than when we came here and I can't wait to get a look inside to see what's causing the weight, but we must get to safety first.

We hustle to catch up to the group ahead of us but they are a good twenty feet further along by the time we reach the soldiers at the exit. My head spins towards them when I hear one of them say, "Last day of this B.S."

I don't stop to ask questions because Abuela is moving faster than a woman her age should be able too. She's closed the distance to fifteen feet from the group when she slows right down. I crane my head to see why and a cold shiver runs down my sweat-soaked back. Boyd's group of men are standing in a line blocking the sidewalk and part of the road. The larger group ahead of us pushes forward but it's clear to me there will be a confrontation. Abuela is now by my side and she takes a hold of the wagon handle with me and starts to guide us across the street. Boyd and his men are now trying to push the group of six down an alleyway but they are pushing back. Most eyes are on them but a couple of his goons start our way when we reach the opposite sidewalk and start to pass them.

I don't know how to play this except to move faster. Abuela has left me to pull the wagon on my own and is fumbling with her messenger bag when I hear a different voice call out.

"Marco, Peter, back up my brother!"

I shoot a look to the confrontation that has turned into a mini brawl before looking for the voice that called out. My eyes lock onto Beck's and he holds my stare for a moment before jutting his chin down the road. He's letting us go. I don't thank him or smile at him, just drop my chin and heave the wagon forward and away. I'm grateful to him for letting us by but that doesn't make him a hero. What he and his brother are doing to the people of this town is monstrous. One good deed doesn't redeem him.

Chapter Three

I watch Claudia and her grandmother rush further down the street to get away from me. I scan the area around them to make sure there are no other gangs around to threaten them before turning back to what my brother and his men are doing. I have to turn my eyes away when I see him push a woman to the ground as he wrenches the ration box from her grasping hands. There's nothing I can do to stop him or help the people he's targeted. I learned a long time ago that I have to be very careful about what battles I pick with Boyd. He might be my only family but that doesn't stop him from having his men give me a beating when he feels I've stepped out of line.

I swear the only thing that keeps me fighting for life in this world is my hatred for him. He's been a bully my whole life but after my father went north to work in the labor camps when I was ten, he really stepped up his game. My mom was too weak with illness to reign him in but she tried to protect me from him as best she could. When she died three years after Dad left, I was completely at his mercy. The only kind thing I can say about Boyd is that he kept me fed on a semi-regular basis, even if it was only the scraps from our ration boxes or ones he'd stolen from others.

He's also the reason I've never been able to have friends. Anyone I've ever shown interest in became a natural target for my brother to harass and bully. I glance over my shoulder to check but the last person I had a real friendship with has disappeared.

"So, you're still sweet on that girl? You let her and the old woman go."

I clench my jaw and turn to face Boyd. I look behind him and see the last of the poor people he's attacked running back the way they'd come empty handed. I take in all the ration boxes and jugs his men are piling on the front stoop of the flower shop and give him a shrug.

"Small fish. We were occupied with a bigger score so I didn't think it was worth the fight." I keep my tone even and hope he buys my explanation. His laugh tells me I failed.

"Sure, little brother. Whatever you say." His eyes dance with malicious amusement. "Your little girlfriend's grown up into a fine-looking woman. She's feisty, too. You man enough to handle that much woman?"

I shake my head in indifference. I know if I show any interest he'll pounce on it and go after her just to torture me. His next words let me know that my tactic no longer works.

"Well good! I fancy a go around with her myself. I'll be keeping my eye out for her in the future." I keep my expression as blank as possible and just raise one shoulder in another shrug. His eyes harden in annoyance that he can't get a rise out of me so he jabs at me a different way.

"Get your ass moving! Haul these boxes into the shop and start inventorying all that we got. You're useless out here anyway."

I don't reply just move to go past him but he grabs my arm in a grip so tight I know I'll be able to count his fingers in bruises later. His voice comes out in a hiss of warning.

"You better start carrying your weight around here, Beck. Me and the boys are getting sick and tired of carrying you around on our backs. You feel me?"

He's talking about how I don't participate in taking down the targets. When forced to go at a group, I'll often pick a woman and then act like a clumsy fool so she can get away or at worst only take a few things from her box so she'll have something to get through the week with.

I give him a sharp nod of understanding and wrench my arm from his grip. There's nothing I'd rather do than carry my own weight right on out of this town and far away from him. The problem is there's nowhere to go. A couple of years ago I had thought about heading north to find my dad or find work in one of the labor camps but word started to get out about the conditions the workers were forced to endure in the camps. I figure one master and a few inches of freedom was better than being controlled twenty-four hours a day by many masters.

By the time I get done sorting the stolen rations and water jugs into the wagons we brought to get it all back to the house, Boyd's ready to call it a day.

He pulls the door open and yells in at me. "Beck, get those wagons out here!"

His men all stand around watching me struggle with getting the overloaded wagons out the door and down the steps to the street. Of course, none of them offer to help, but they enjoy making taunting comments on my every move. By the time I get the last wagon out to the street, Boyd's lost interest in the game and is fuming with impatience. He sends me a look of contempt and then points to Marco.

"Go do a last sweep of the square for any stragglers and then catch up. The rest of you, grab a wagon and let's go. I'm ready to eat!"

I look down at the last two wagons left for me to pull on my own and am not even remotely surprised to see that they're the heaviest ones filled with the water jugs. I let out a deep sigh and bend down to get the handles. There's got to be a better life out there for me, somewhere.

Chapter Four

When we reach the intersection to Silvia's house, Abuela waves us past it. I'm out of breath from the pace and weight of the wagon so I can't question her. It's probably better to get the wagon safely home first anyway. I can run back for Glo after it's secured. The predators are only focusing on the stations so we should be safe enough if we are quick.

By the time we reach the house I'm desperate for water. My mouth and throat feel like the desert that surrounds us has invaded. There's no way I can lug or lift the wagon up the stairs so I pull it around the side of the house to the back door. Abuela rushes ahead of me and into the house but she's back quickly with a large glass of water. I take it from her gratefully but only allow myself a few swallows before trying to hand it back. She pushes my hand and the glass back at me and I can't help but look over towards the well. I don't know if I have the energy to pump anymore today.

"DÍA! Forget the well! Drink it all and then help me get this beast inside."

I compromise by chugging half the water in the glass down before thrusting it back at her.

"You drink the rest!"

She's forced to take it from me or it will spill so I turn away from her and heave the wagon up the one step at the back door and into the kitchen. I'd like to say it's cooler in the house but it's not. The only difference is that the sun isn't beaming down on my head. I leave the wagon still covered and rush deeper into the house to the atrium. Full sun is beaming down onto my poor plants and I want to cry at my stupid mistake. I should have pulled the curtains before we left. It's part of my routine but that got all messed up with the station run and I forgot. I can only hope that none of the plants die from my error. I back out of the room once the curtains have shut out the sun and wearily trudge back to the kitchen. I will be pumping water today after all. If I want the plants to survive then they'll need another watering.

When I reach the kitchen, I find Abuela moving quickly to empty the wagon of rations. I'm still surprised at her energy after she was confined to her bed for so long. She's stacking everything on the counter but not putting anything away into the cupboards. I glance over to the table and want nothing more than to sink down onto one of the chairs with the faded yellow cushions, even though they are paper thin from years of use. I sigh and look away. I need to help get all this put away, fetch Gloria, and then start pumping for water. Everything else on my list will have to be bumped to tomorrow.

Abuela places a bag of rice onto the counter, turns and sees me standing in the doorway. She looks down into the half empty wagon and gives a curt nod before coming over and taking my arm. She guides me over to the table and motions towards a chair. I shake my head.

"No, I can't. There are too many things to get done. If I sit now, I might not get up."

She points at a chair with a stern finger. "Sit! We have things to discuss now while Gloria is not here."

It only takes me a half second to cave in. As much as the rest will do me good, answers will be better. She settles across from me and folds her hands in front of her on the table.

"Día, we must prepare to leave this place."

I bark out a surprised laugh. That was the last thing I expected her to say.

"Sure, and just where do you think we should go? How about the North Pole? I would love to see snow! Glo could build a snowman!"

The look I received for my sarcasm has me shrinking down in the chair and looking away in shame. She just keeps pinning me to the chair with that look until a meek, "I'm sorry," squeaks out of me.

"Claudia, you must listen now. Your lives may depend on it! It's not just the well I'm talking about. This town has been on its death bed for years but the funeral will happen tomorrow. The stations are closing! There will be no more food or water for the people here and that's when things will become the most dangerous. You and your sister must leave before that happens!"

I open my mouth to argue with her but pause as flashes from earlier fill my brain. The man saying to make the rations last. Asking if she understood why. The soldier saying "last day". I know she's right. They aren't coming back. That means...My eyes flare wide as the realization sinks in. It will be chaos once word gets out. The station riot will be nothing compared to what's coming. She reaches out and grips my hands.

"You see? They will search for food and water everywhere. No place will be safe. You must be gone before that begins!"

I start shaking my head. "But where? Where can we go? And why do you keep saying me and Gloria? You must come too!"

"Yes, I will come too, but I do not know how far I will get with you. I feel Him calling me Home to Heaven. Your Abuelo is waiting for me there, but first, he has sent me a dream to get you and your sister to safety." She shakes a finger at me when my expression fills with doubt. "Don't look at me like that! I'm old but I'm not senile! The dream was just a reminder of where we should go to find salvation." I nod slowly for her to continue but I'm still concerned she's losing her faculties.

"You know your Abuelo was a prospector? You remember the stories I used to tell you about his adventures? He did quite well for us. He built this house and we had a very nice amount of money in the bank from all his mining claims. But the one thing he always wanted was for us to live in his secret garden, his 'jardín del paraíso'. It was a hidden valley he stumbled upon in the Black Mountains of Arizona. He said there was no evidence that any other human had ever been there. Lush with vegetation from a natural spring! It was his dream for us to live there in peace and raise a family away from all the troubles of the world. He showed me pictures of it and the small house he built by hand for us." She looks down at her hands and shakes her head sadly. "He gave that dream up for me when your Mother was born. I couldn't imagine living in such isolation with an infant. I felt the need to be near doctors and other families so she would have playmates. He never said a word but I know it broke his heart. When he didn't come back from the desert the last time, I thought maybe he had gone there to live out his dream. I was relieved when they found his body but so sad because I could no longer pretend he was alive and living where he wanted to be."

I leave her lost in memories for a few moments and wonder why I had never heard this story before. It doesn't take long for her to straighten up.

"So, this is where we will go! There are no bandits or gangs to plague us and there is plenty of water to grow more crops. The wildlife flock to the valley so there will be meat to hunt. Yes, this is where we will go!" She pushes away from the table and rises to her feet. "Come, there is much to prepare for the journey."

I stay seated and look up at her, feeling both bemused and frustrated.

"Abuela, it sounds like a lovely dream but how do even know if it's there and even if it was, how are we supposed to get there? We are surrounded by desert! Do you really want me to drag a nine-year-old child out into that on a vague memory of a place that might not even exist?"

Her hands hit her hips and a scowl crossed her face. "You think I would suggest this on a whim? I know it's there! I've seen the pictures he brought back. He described it so vividly, I could feel the cool mist from the waterfall on my face." Her hands fell to her sides and her shoulders slumped. "Día, we have three choices. Go to one of the labor farms and be little more than a slave for one meal and one cup of water a day and then die. Stay here and face attack, starvation, and death by dehydration and die. OR take a chance for a life in paradise. Yes, it will be hard and dangerous but of the three options, it's the only one with a possibility of life!"

I lower my head in defeat. There is no happy ending open to us. "Show me this picture," I say in a voice that is almost a whisper.

I hear her shuffle away but keep my head down, imagining all the futures we face. I can see Glo's withered body as she toils at manual labor in the camps. I see her lying in a pool of blood after looters break in to steal the little food we have. And then I see her slowly being covered by sand in the middle of the desert when we don't find the paradise Abuela speaks of. Not once can I picture her laughing beside a waterfall of clean, cool water.

When she returns and tosses three pictures onto the table in front of me, I reach for them with no hope left in my soul. The pictures are thinner than paper, blurred, and faded with age. I can still see the waterfall she speaks of that falls into a large pool before it turns into a stream. There's one taken from above of the valley that shows the house she says my Abuelo built for her with the waterfall and pool beside it. It's bigger than I thought it would be with a front veranda that runs the length of it with rocking chairs on it. The last picture is of a small group of what looks like deer drinking from the stream. I drop the pictures back to the table and look up at her.

"It's beautiful but if it's so remote and untouched then how did he get the building materials there? If there's a road in, someone else would have found it."

She pulls out a chair and sits. "No, no road! He took it all in with a hover sled train." At my confused expression, she explains. "We used to have amazing technology. The things we were capable of were like miracles! After the water wars, it all went away. Only the people in the north have the tech now. A hover sled was a machine that could carry heavy loads over the ground on a cushion of air. They used to be used regularly but I haven't seen one in use for over twenty years." She looks out the window to the back yard. "We have one."

I huff out a laugh. I'm pretty sure I would have noticed such a miracle machine at some point in the last seventeen years that I've lived here. So, all I mockingly say is, "Really?"

The scowl is back on her face. "Día! You have become cynical and disrespectful! I asked you to trust me. I think the eighty-two years of life I've lived has earned me that."

My eyes drop in shame. She's right, I have become jaded to life in the last month of managing things myself. She doesn't deserve this attitude from me.

"Abuela, I am sorry for my behavior. There is no excuse other than I am scared of what's to come."

She reaches out and grasps my hand. "I understand, it looks bleak but I believe in what I'm telling you. Please, Día, believe in me." At my tearful nod, she continues. "There is a hover sled hidden in the old workshop at the back of the property. It was your grandfather's. The only reason they found his body was because the sled was there beside the chasm he fell into. They used it to bring his body back to me for burial. It will need to be brought out and placed in the sun to charge so it's ready to go tonight. We will load it with the supplies you will need for the trip and to get started in the valley once you arrive."

Inside, I don't believe any of it but I will play along out of respect.

"So we will float on this machine to the secret valley?"

She pulls her hands from mine and pulls a tattered paper from her apron pocket.

"No, it doesn't work like that. Gloria may be able to travel on it for brief periods but the weight placement will need to be balanced."

I have no idea what these words mean so I just nod and lean forward to look at the delicate paper she's unfolding onto the table. I'm surprised to see that it's a faded map. A dim splash of blue and green in the corner shows what I assume is the location of this paradise.

"This will show you the way once you get close enough. It is very far from here, hundreds of miles, but there is a way to make such a journey manageable. First, you must stay far away from any road. You would be a bright blinking target if anyone saw you with supplies and such coveted working technology. Instead, you will travel as Abuelito did, on the old train tracks! He was always so paranoid that someone would follow him to one of his claims that he never traveled by road. The tracks haven't been used by ground trains since I was a young woman. They retired them when the sky trains were invented but the tracks are still in place. Abuelito used them to get closer to his claims and then hiked in the rest of the way. That's why he chose this location to build our home. The tracks run behind our property. He would always leave either late at night or very early in the morning."

My mouth drops open in disbelief. "Are you saying we have a train too?"

She snorts a laugh at me and shakes her head like I'm a foolish child. "No, that would be ridiculous. It would be too big to conceal, too loud to go unnoticed and it would need fuel to run."

I nod my head in serious agreement. Of course, that makes no sense. It's nothing like a magical machine that floats on air!

"So we will walk on the tracks with the floating machine following behind us, then?"

A slow smile spreads across her face. "No, you will be taking Abuelito's favorite toy, his Mathilda. He called it his workhorse. It is a very special rail handcart that he had shipped from Japan!"

I just have to shake my head. I've lived here since I was one-year old. All these magical things she's talking about don't exist. I would have seen them at some point in my life. My poor Abuela's mind has slipped back into some distant past. I felt drained of all hope. I wouldn't be able to count on her help now for what to do next.

She must see it in my expression because her face turns sad and she pulls me to my feet.

"Come, there is so much to do and we will need to collect your sister first."

I follow her out the back door and take a few steps to the right to go around the house and out to the street to fetch Gloria but she heads deeper into the back yard. I let out a sigh and follow after her. The sun has reached high noon and it's not safe for us to be out for long without protection. As she reaches the back of our property, she angles toward a section of the fence and starts pulling away the dry and brittle branches of what used to be a six-foot privacy hedge. I catch up to her and even though I feel we are wasting time, help her snap off the branches. I'm mildly surprised when a gate appears as more branches are removed. She frees a strange padlock from the final stems and pushes raised buttons that release the lock. I've never seen such a lock that didn't require a key before and I want to take a closer look but she's pulled the gate open and hurried through it. There's ten feet of level land before it dips into a drainage ditch that hasn't seen water in decades.

I marvel at how quickly she is moving for a woman of her age as she plows ahead, down and then back up the ditch. On the other side, I see an old building with no windows that looks like it will fall down at any moment. I follow her around to the front where there are two huge doors and end up on my knees when I trip on a rock. On my hands and knees, my face only a foot from the dusty ground I see a line in the sand. My hand moves forward and brushes the sand away revealing a dull metal bar. I slowly turn my head following the line in the sand and see it runs right under the doors of the building. I turn my head to look the other way and see the lines connect with a slightly elevated set of train tracks. I stare at those tracks as something starts to stir in my chest.

When I hear the sound of boards falling to the ground I push back up onto my feet and turn to help Abuela remove the long boards that have been stacked up against the doors. Once the last board topples to the side it reveals another of those weird locks. She pushes the buttons again and I find myself holding my breath as she swings one of the huge doors open so the light shines in and seems to spotlight what has been hidden inside. Everything is covered in dust and sand that has seeped in over the long years but it's clear what I'm looking at. My breath whooshes out as I step forward and past Abuela, who's smiling in triumph, towards our ticket out of here.

Chapter Five

I've never seen a real train in my life but I have seen children's books with cartoon versions of them. What waits inside of the building is a mini version of what I think a train car should be. It's not much more than seven or eight feet in length and around five feet across. It's completely enclosed with the top half all windows. I move slowly around it looking for some kind of engine to propel it but don't see anything so I find the door and pull it open. It's an easy step up and into it. There is a padded bench along one side and shelving that runs on the other. Right in the center is a triangle frame of metal with two levers on either side. Abuela climbs in behind me and pats one of the levers.

"Good thing you have a lifetime of practice with pumping the well!" I give her a confused look so she explains. "This is how you get it to move. You pump it and it turns the wheels. There is a small engine underneath that will store a charge from the pumping and also some solar panels on the roof to gather energy. It will let you take breaks and keep moving but it doesn't last more than a few hours at a time. It can run between ten and fifteen miles per hour depending on how much you put into pumping but the engine will go faster, around twenty-five miles an hour. It's not that fast but it will eat up the miles faster than you could walk, it's quiet, and it will give you shelter from the sun during the day and somewhere to rest at night."

I just stare at her thinking about all she's told me and how I thought she was losing her mind. I take another quick look around before asking, "Show me the flying sled?"

Her laughter peels out like water. "It's not magic, Día and it doesn't fly." She starts explaining about something called downward air thrust but my eyes must have glazed over because she stops midsentence and waves the rest of the explanation away. "Come, I will show you how to use the controls from the panel and then I will need your help to get the sled outside into the sun to charge."

I watch closely as she shows me a hidden panel with switches and buttons in the floor of the cart in one corner and then follow her off of the cart. Leaning against the wall of the far side of the building is something covered by a tarp thick with dust and sand. When we pull it off it creates such a cloud that we are forced to run out the door until it settles and we can breathe again. When we can safely return, I'm totally let down by the machine she has told me about. It's nothing more than a flat-topped, thick platform with rails around the top and rubber bumpers around the edges. When we tilt it away from the wall, I peek behind it but all I see is metal circles covering the bottom. It's way too heavy for us to lift so we drag it across the floor, out the door and around the side of the building into the full sun. We carefully lower it down so it lays flat and I watch as she flicks latches at every corner until the rubber bumpers drop open. She shows me how the solar panels are folded up accordion style and how they pull open to fan out a good three feet on every side of the sled to soak up the power-giving sun. The irony of the sun that is slowly killing us making it possible for us to get somewhere safe is not lost on me.

Before closing the building up and going to retrieve Gloria, she runs me through the controls on a remote for the sled and how to fold it all back up so it will be ready to travel. She places the remote face down so the small solar charger on the back of it will face the sun. Before we leave, I climb up the slight incline to the tracks and take a good look both ways. I'm nervous that someone will stumble upon our sled and steal it before we've even had a chance to use it but every direction is deserted. There's no reason anyone would be out here on the outskirts of town.

I'm still in awe that everything she has told me seems to be true. I'm starting to have hope now that there's a way out for us. We hit the backyard and she secures the gate before turning to me.

"I have another map of the rail lines I will give you to take. It very important that you pay attention to where they split. You must take the third junction and continue to go east. Once you get to Coyote Rock you stop and change to the secret map. From there you will go on foot the rest of the journey. Día, I cannot stress enough that you don't take any of the other junctions! They will all lead you to what were once major cities. Those cities are full of evil. The devil owns them now."

I nod in understanding of her warning but am concerned that she keeps excluding herself for the plans.

"Abuela, you will be with us the whole way!"

She reaches up and cups my cheek with a withered hand.

"I would love if that were the truth but my dream also showed me that today will be my last day on this unforgiving earth. Día, I dreamed of fire! You must get your sister to safety no matter what happens tonight. Promise me!"

I clasp my hand over hers tightly. "It was just a dream! You will be with us when we find this paradise."

She pulls her hand away and grabs me by my shoulders with a little shake. "I hope that's true but if not, you **will** leave without me, for Gloria's sake!"

I don't want to humor her on this but there is much to do, so I just nod and then pull her into a fierce hug. She grips me just as tight and whispers in my ear.

"You make me so proud. I'm honored that you were my child to raise, know and love."

She pushes me away and turns to the house, calling over her shoulder as she goes.

"Go get your sister. I will start preparing the supplies. Be careful and no word of this to Silvia!"

I want to argue that we should warn them of what's coming but the screen door slaps and she is gone. I make my way around the house and head towards the center of town. My thoughts are full of everything I've learned and seen today. I glance up at the sun and wince at the heat and brightness of it before pulling my scarves further over my head. It's hard to believe that the day is only an hour or so past noon. There are only four or five hours left before darkness falls and we can start loading up all we will need. I feel slightly shell shocked by the change of our circumstances. It feels like minutes ago I was pumping the well in despair. I'm so caught up in my thoughts that I don't even see the group coming toward me before I hear them.

"Indigo, Indigo! What a treat for me to see you twice in one day. It was very rude of you not to stop for a conversation with me on your way back from the stations. But I forgive you, I was, after all, …occupied with another matter."

I refuse to speak to this jackal of a man so I just stare him down and wait for what he will say next. I hold myself rock stiff as he scans my body from head to toe even though I can feel the tremor of fear wanting to break free. I won't give him the satisfaction of seeing my fear.

"Look at you, all grown up, proud and strong. I like that in a woman. I've been considering settling down lately. You are just the kind of girl I would do such a thing for." He's smirking at my discomfort as his pack of thugs laugh and shove each other. "You even have some nice curves. Most of the women left in this town are nothing more than stick figures." His eyes narrow as he looks me over again, this time with suspicion and I feel a bolt of real fear flow through me. We might not have a lot of food but I know we have way more than most. He may be coming to the same conclusion. My eyes finally leave his as I look to Beck but he's not looking at me. He's glaring at his brother with such hatred and loathing I'm surprised that Boyd doesn't go up in flames. My attention is brought back to him when he speaks again. This time his tone isn't soft and menacing but hard and sure.

"I think now would be a good time to have that conversation."

I swallow hard and brace myself to run but just as he lifts his hand to grab me, an urgent voice calls out his name causing him to turn away.

"Boyd! Boyd, you're not going to believe what I just heard at the station! This is major!"

He waves his arm to all his men to move off down the intersection that goes away from where I need to go. He turns just his head back in my direction and the coldness I see in them has me sucking in a breath.

"To be continued…soon."

I don't move a muscle as they all walk away and turn the corner. Once they are out of sight, I double over with my hands on my knees and gasp for breath. He's coming for us. I could read it in his eyes! We have to go. We have to escape before he and his men come for us. I have a very good notion of just what his man learned at the station and once they start planning for a life without rations, they will come for everyone else's. I surge upright and dash forward. I have to get Gloria and get back to the house. I can't help but peek around the corner to make sure the gang is far enough away before sprinting across the street but I keep my head turned to watch their backs, afraid they will change their minds and come for me now. My heart misses a beat when one of the men at the very back of their pack turns and looks my way but I realize that it's Beck watching me so I keep going.

I'm surprised that he has so much hate for his brother in him, but then again, I haven't known his mind since we were children. My feet fly the rest of the way to Silvia's where I collect Gloria but I'm too out of breath to have much of a conversation. I wave goodbye and thank her for watching my sister before I practically pull Gloria down the street. When we leave Silvia's street she finally manages to pull her arm out of my tight grip.

"Día, stop! I can't go so fast!"

I don't want to scare her but it's time for her to know a few things. "You must, Glo! I have been stopped by gangs twice today. It's not safe out here. We have to get home as quick as we can!"

I feel horrible as her eyes widen in fear and she looks all around like monsters are about to jump out and snatch her. Sadly, there are monsters and they could show up at any moment.

"Come on Glo, we don't have to run but we must be very quick, ok?"

She nods, her eyes brimming with tears, and slides her small hand into mine. When we make it back to our street without seeing anyone else, I send a quick prayer of thanks up to the God I don't believe in, just in case. I send her up the stairs to her room to get cleaned up and changed as I head further into the house. I head straight for the atrium. I tell myself that it's to check the soil dampness but I know it won't matter after today. They will all be dead once I'm gone. Other than my family and survival, the plants have been the only thing that I've cared about since I was a tiny girl. There's never been anything in my life that I could do to make things better in this world. But my plants, I could tend them and nurse them and see them flourish into something good. I hope I will be able to grow more if we make it to the valley.

I push the door open and the sheer destruction has me falling to my knees in physical pain. There is soil covering the floor with most of the pots overturned. All the fruit and vegetables have been taken, there are only leaves and stems with roots exposed laying in discarded piles. My eyes flash to the corner but both of my small trees are gone, pots and all. A low moan escapes me at what I've lost but my next thought is for my family. I'm too late! Boyd's gang has beaten me here. I have to find my family and try to protect them!

I use the door frame to pull myself to my feet and hurtle down the hall to the kitchen. I come flying to a stop at what I find there. Abuela is at the table with an open wooden chest. She is wrapping plant cuttings in damp rags before rolling them up in cut up sheets and placing them into the chest. I let my eyes wander the rest of the room, still in shock. There are canvas bags piled by the door with the missing harvest peeking out and next to them stand the pots with my small trees in them. I heave out a half sob causing Abuela to turn my way with an apologetic expression. She comes over and guides me to the table where she pushes me down into a chair.

"I'm so sorry, Día. I knew you wouldn't be able to do it so I took that burden from you. But look, look - I have cuttings from every plant. They will last in this chest as long as you give them a little water every day. Once you get to the valley, you will replant them and have twice as many to tend! This will all be a new, better start for you and your sister. Let the past go and look to the future."

I nod my head in agreement but I still need a few minutes to accept all these changes so I just sit and watch as she finishes wrapping the last plant cuttings and places them in the chest. She closes the lid and latches it before patting it gently.

"Here is your future. Protect them well." She turns to me and pulls me from the chair. "I need your help for the next part. I still have some strength but my knees are not what they used to be."

I let her lead me to the rarely used door that leads down into the basement under the house. It's been a few months since I've been down these steps. There's nothing of value that I know of stored down there as we eat everything almost as soon as we get it from rations or our plants. There are only three small cots that we use to sleep on a few months of the year and some old shelving. Halfway down the steps, I feel the temperature start to lower. By the time I hit the bottom, I'm closing my eyes and breathing in the earthy tang that fills the air as a delicious feeling of coolness rushes across my body. I can't remember the last time I felt this way. It's an amazing feeling that I want to enjoy for a few minutes so I ignore the noise Abuela is making as she moves things around over on one of the walls. It is never this cool down here in the summer months and I didn't realize it would be this cool during the rest of the year or I would have come down here every day. When she calls for me, I think about ignoring her. I think about just laying down on the hard-packed ground and sleeping right there, cool for the first time in my life but I know just how much there still is to do. Boyd's hard eyes flash across my thoughts and that's all it takes to get me moving again.

My tiny Abuela is trying to move a large shelving unit away from the wall so I rush over and pull her away before getting a good grip and swinging it away from the wall. At some point, while I was wallowing in the air temperature, she has lit an old glass lantern. She holds it up and squeezes past me to get to the wall. I'm surprised when what I thought was hard-packed soil turns out to be a sheet, colored to look like the soil. She tugs hard on it until it drops away and then lifts the lantern up to light what's been concealed behind it.

At first, I don't understand, then I don't believe it but I rush towards it anyway and run my hands over jug after jug of what looks like water. When I can finally tear my eyes away from all that precious liquid, I turn to her and whisper, "How?"

She looks past me with satisfaction. "Eighty-two years, I've learned a thing or two! This, this I started when you were just a tiny girl after we lost the water wars. I knew there might come a time when the well would dry up so I built in a safety net. I used to rotate them out regularly but I had to stop around ten years ago. My knees just wouldn't take the stairs anymore. So, the water will be stale and probably have a plastic taste to it but it will keep you alive until you get to the valley."

She turns to meet my eyes and gives me a devilish grin. "Start hauling!"

Chapter Six

By the time I've hauled up ten jugs, the cool air no longer feels good. Instead, it makes the sweat on my body cold and clammy. I pause as I leave the jugs by the back door and try and calculate just how much water three people in the middle of the desert would need. I have no idea how long it will take us to get to the valley so it's impossible to calculate. I don't think we will need as much while we're in the handcart but once we start on foot, we'll go through it faster. Shaking my head, I turn and head back down the stairs. It's better to have too much than not enough. Space will be an issue but I can hang the jugs from the sides of the car if necessary and we can discard some of the jugs once they're empty. Except for a small bag of clothes and personal items, all we are taking is food, water, and the plant clippings as well as her medical box and a few household things. Abuela says that the house has everything we need from when her husband built it, so hopefully she's right, or I'll need to learn how to make household goods from scratch. I try and picture myself making furniture or casting pots but that's outside my skill set so I have no choice but to go on faith that there will be what we need there.

I haul up six more jugs before Abuela pushes me into a chair at the table and places a plate with leftover tortillas filled with bean sprouts and protein paste that we got in our ration boxes. The paste has no taste at all to it but the dried spices she makes from our herb garden give it a nice flavor. I watch her as I eat. She's busy at the kitchen counter making up more filled tortillas and wrapping them in used paper and then clothes for the trip. I scan the kitchen and feel weary with exhaustion at all the piles of supplies that need to be moved across the yard and out to the handcart. It's already been a long day with the afternoon coming to its end so I try and brace myself for a long evening of loading supplies and then an even longer night of pumping the cart to get us away.

I'm distracted by Gloria bouncing into the room. I try not to smile at her complete look of shock at the state of the kitchen. Her eyes fly to mine with a look of confusion.

"What's going on? Where did all this come from?"

I push out a chair with my foot and wave her into it. I don't want to scare her but she needs to at least be aware of what's coming.

"We're going on an adventure! Things are happening in town that are making it too dangerous for us to stay here so we are moving to a new home." Her little face crumples in despair so I add some spin to it. "We have a treasure map that will lead us to a secret paradise garden that has a waterfall and a pond you can swim in! For the first part of the journey, we get to travel in a train car and then we will use a flying sled to carry all our belongings. Doesn't that sound like an amazing adventure?"

Her face changes to wonder but just as quickly turns suspicious. "You're making that up!"

I shake my head. "No, I'm not. It's all true but it will be hard and maybe dangerous so I need to be able to count on your help. Do you think you're up for it?"

She bounces in her seat with excitement. "YES! I can help. I can do anything you want! I'm not a little girl anymore, you can count on me! Are we going to where Mama is?"

I try not to change my expression at the question. She doesn't remember our mother. She was only one when Mama left us but Gloria has always hoped that she would come back for us.

"No, we are going somewhere else. We must leave tonight. The gangs are going to be breaking into houses and stealing food and water from people soon. We have to be gone before then. It's important that you don't leave the house without one of us with you." Her expression has turned from excited to nervous. "It's ok, we have some time before they come but we have to hurry so I need you to go up to your room and pack a bag. Four sets of clothes and a few treasures you want to take."

She nods and bites her lip before asking, "Will we ever come back here?"

I shrug my shoulders. "I don't know, Glo. Maybe one day if things get better."

Her bottom lip trembles slightly but then firms up and she gives a sharp nod before jumping up and running out of the room. I close my eyes in sadness for a moment as I hear her thunder up the stairs before looking over to Abuela. She looks as sad as I feel.

"I'm sorry, Claudia. I'm sorry that you've had to be both mother and sister to Gloria. It's not fair to either of you. I wish I had raised a stronger daughter. Your grandfather and I tried for years to have children and we had given up when Monica surprised us. I was already in my forties when she was born and she was such a blessing that we spoiled her. She was so young when her father died that I don't think I raised her to be strong enough to do the right thing by you girls. I'm sorry, you both deserve better."

I push to my feet and cross the room, pulling her into a hug. "We have you. That's the biggest blessing of all."

She pats my back a few times before gently pushing me away and then wipes at her eyes before changing the subject.

"Bring a few more jugs up while I go get the sled, it should be charged by now. We'll start transferring the supplies out to the handcart."

I'm surprised by that so I ask, "You really think it's charged up already?"

She nods. "Yes, two hours in direct sun will fully charge it to run for eight hours. The heavier the load the less run time it will give you, though."

"Oh, then we should leave it until it's time to leave or it won't run all night. I can carry all this out there myself."

She shakes her head with a smile. "No, we will use the sled to ferry everything out there to the cart, not to haul it down the track! There is a small trailer that attaches to the back of the cart. We will put the supplies in it and inside the cart. The sled then sits on top of the trailer. You will only use it once you stop and have to go on foot to the valley. The charge wouldn't last long enough to travel that far on the tracks."

We go our separate ways to our tasks as I think of all the things I don't know how to do as far as logistics go to make this trip a success. I'm just thankful she will be with us to guide me. I bring up more jugs but take them straight outside to the backyard this time. Gloria joins me with her small bag of possessions so I put her to work carrying out some of the lighter boxes and bags while I run upstairs and fill my own bag. The clothes are the easy part to pick out. Some of my favorite books go into the bag but then I stall. What else do I want to take? There are a few old pictures that I grab but my hand hovers over the only picture I have of my mother. I had just turned ten the day she walked out and never came back. I let one finger drift down to the top of the frame and slowly pull until she crashes face first to the dresser. We are leaving this place for a new life and she will never be a part of it.

By the time I make it back to the kitchen, Abuela is back with the sled and she and Gloria are loading supplies on it. I'm amazed at the quiet humming it makes and can't help laying down on the ground to look under it. I feel the air it's displacing against my face and understand its workings a little better but it still seems a little like magic to me. I get to my feet and blush in embarrassment at the look and eye roll Abuela sends my way but Gloria is laughing and clapping her hands so I take it in stride. We pile as much as we can on it but there is still more to take. I worry that we'll have to abandon much of it once we are forced to go on foot but I'd rather do that than leave it for the gangs to fight over.

Abuela hands me the remote control and guides me through the motions to get the sled moving. Gloria dashes ahead of us and through the gate. This is such an adventure for her. Like me, she didn't even know there was more to the property other than the yard. I'm impressed with how the sled manages the dry ditch, thinking it would tip over but I hear the humming increase so it must compensate somehow. Once we reach the old building, she shows me how to lower and shut the sled off. I'm still standing beside it marveling at how we can transfer so much weight without breaking our backs when I hear Gloria squeal in glee. I turn around in time to see her climb up into the cart and disappear inside it.

Abuela waves me over and shows me the brakes on the wheels and how to unlatch them manually. She says there's a control to apply them inside but I need to know as much as I can about how the machine works. I'm still annoyed that she keeps excluding herself from the journey but I will save that fight for if it's needed when we leave. She calls Gloria off the cart and takes us around to the back of it where we all push to get it moved ahead and halfway out the doors. The wheels make the most agonizing screech as they move for the first time in three decades. We throw the front brakes on and Abuela searches the shelves until she comes back with a rusted oil can. The oil she squirts onto the wheels and axels is thick as slime with age but she seems to think it will still work.

Once again, we work as a team to attach the small trailer, that is the exact same size as the hover sled, to the back of the cart and then we begin transferring the supplies to it. Abuela insists that all the water jugs and as much of the food as possible go onto the shelves inside the cart. It's going to be a tight fit for all three of us in the handcart with everything were taking but there will be enough room for two of us to stretch out on the bench with one of us pumping the handle. Even with the new vigor Abuela is showing, I know most of the pumping will fall on me. I'm ok with that knowing it will be worth all the pain and exhaustion once we get to the valley. I'm fully committed to this trip now and I've closed the door on all the doubts

I have about it really being out there. I have no choice but to believe. There are no other options open to us.

When we have emptied the sled and start our return to the house for the rest of the supplies, I'm surprised to see that the sun is close to the horizon. The day has been so long but also feels like it's gone too fast. We're leaving this place in an hour or so. The only home my sister and I have ever know known. I find my feet slowing as we enter the yard and I take in the weathered wood of the house. So many memories are stored behind its walls. Some bad, my mother always unhappy and constantly fighting with Abuela. Then her leaving and me waiting by the front window for her to come back. But even more are happy. Gloria being born right there in that house and being thrilled to be a big sister. Abuela teaching me how to cook and tend to our precious plants. Teaching Gloria to read, word by word on the front porch. These are all things I will have to say goodbye to now.

I shake off my nostalgia and move faster to help load the last of the water jugs as Glo struggles to lift the wooden chest of plant clippings. I see her determination so leave her to it. She might be tiny but she has strength in her small arms. Abuela walks towards the house calling out to us,

"Finish this last bit and I will go gather what's left in the kitchen. I put the food I prepared for us in the basement to keep cool. I'll go get it and then we will be ready to leave. Say goodbye to our home, girls. She's been good to us!"

Chapter Seven

The house my brother took over a few years ago is one of the biggest in the town. It was previously owned by a wealthy family that had fled north before the wall went up and had been sitting empty for years. He not only picked it for the size and grandeur of it but because it had an antique hand pump connected to a well in what was once a decorative garden. The previous owners probably had it installed for a quaint water feature. For us, it meant life.

The house is big enough to hold all his men. Boyd likes having them all under his roof to better control them. When we had gotten all the wagons into the front entrance, they all left them there for me to unpack and they settled in, lounging on old dusty couches in the living room. That suits me just fine. I'm pumped full of rage at the way Boyd had threatened Claudia and was ready to gut him like a fish if he spoke to me. I'm getting a grip on some of the jugs to carry them into the kitchen when Marco's excited voice rings out and Boyd yells for everyone to "shut up". I let the jugs fall back into the wagon and step closer to the livingroom entrance to hear what he had to say.

"Alright, Marco. Start at the beginning." Boyd commands.

"Right, so I go back to the square like you said and take a good look around. It's not like normal where they leave the tables and partitions in place for next week. They're pulling it all down and loading it up into the trucks. They even took the signs down! Instead, they put up new ones. So once the soldiers cleared out and the trucks left, I ran over to see what the new signs said.

You're not going to believe it! They're shutting the whole thing down. No more rations or water…at all! The sign says there will be buses coming next week instead to take everyone north to the camps. The government's abandoning all the southwestern states completely!"

I peek around the corner to see into the room and watch as Boyd's eyes go from rage to cold and calculating at the information. He spits onto the wood floor between his feet and snarls.

"No one's taking me to any labor camp! What about the rest of you? You wanna go be some government big shot's slave?" When all the men roar in the negative he leans back. "This is a game changer. If we're going to survive without access to the ration stations then we're going to have to take matters into our own hands and start stocking up right now." He looks around and yells, "Somebody get me a map of town!" Once he has one spread out on the dirty table in front of him, they start marking occupied houses street by street.

I slip away from the door and go back to moving the supplies into the kitchen as my thoughts spin out of control. I don't want to go to a camp either but I definitely don't want to be around here when Boyd and his thugs burn the place to the ground. I know that's what's coming with his planning. They're going to go house to house and force everyone to give up what little they have. People are going to get hurt. He won't hold back now that he knows his supply chain is about to go dry.

I finish up quickly, grab a tall glass of water from one of the stolen jugs and head out the side door to the back yard to think. I like sitting out here after the sun has passed over the house and there's a little bit of shade. I settle into an old wooden lawn chair and try to ignore the ugly voices floating out of the open windows as they compare notes on who lives where and what they might have. I chug back my water and then rest my head back and close my eyes. I can't be a part of this. I can't go loot people's homes of the little they have left, especially when I know there won't be more coming. I wish there was some way I could warn the town of what was coming and then find a way to escape this place. I'm so sick of being trapped here under Boyd's thumb. I want to run. Run far away and find a new life but there just isn't anywhere left to go. I feel all hope leave me when I realize I'm going to die in this town.

"…here first! Anyone else notice she seemed a little too well fed? I bet they have food stored up in that house." Floats out through the window to me. I sit up as fear for my once friend fills me, but what I hear next changes my fear to determination.

"The girl's mine. I don't care what you do to the old woman or the brat, but no one lays a hand on the girl!"

I might die in this town but I'll go out doing the right thing, protecting the last person who showed me kindness!

Chapter Eight

Gloria and I have just finished loading the last jug and box onto the sled when a massive banging noise comes from inside of the house. My head whips towards the back door in fear. Did we wait too long? Are the gangs here? I push Gloria down to the ground beside the sled.

"Wait here! Do not move until I tell you it's safe and if I yell for you to run, you get out that gate and into the handcart. I will meet you there!"

I don't wait for her agreement but turn and sprint for the door just as another loud pounding comes. I'm so frantic with worry for Abuela that I yank the screen door out of its top hinges. I'm halfway through the kitchen with a direct line of sight to the front door so I see the moment it crashes open. There's a tall man silhouetted in the opening but I can't make out who it is. When he yells my name and rushes towards me down the hall, I recognize the voice instantly.

"Claudia!" Beck bellows down the hall.

The fear I felt a moment ago morphs into indignation and I bellow right back at him.

"How dare you break into my house? What do you think you're doing? Did your brother send you to harass me again?"

He rushes right up to me and I see how his chest is heaving for air like he's just run miles. His voice is a rough rasp as he grabs my arm while trying to catch his breath.

"No…time…they're…coming…for…YOU! Have…to…run!"

My body goes cold with terror. I don't know why he's crossed his brother to warn me but he's right, we have to run, right now. I yank my arm from his and spin towards the back door. I can feel his breath on the back of my next as he follows me right out the door.

"Gloria! Take the sled back to the cart. We have to go right now!"

I see her face pale in the last of the day's light but she doesn't move. She's staring at who's behind me.

"Never mind him! He came to warn us that the gangs are heading this way. I need you to go and start loading as much as you can lift so we can escape. I will get Abuela and meet you there."

Beck steps around me and looks the sled over before turning to me. He's gotten his breathing under control when he speaks but I'm shocked at his words.

"You're already running? You have somewhere to go? Can I come too? I can help!"

I shake my head in confusion. Does he want to come with us? He hasn't spoken to me since we were children. Why would he want to come with me anywhere? I remember the look of pure hate he flashed at his brother and how he let us pass after we got our rations. Maybe Beck isn't as bad as I thought and he's looking to escape too. A shout from the front of the house in the street rings out making all of my thoughts about Beck disappear. I can't deal with him now. I have to get Abuela and run! I point at Gloria.

"GO, take the sled as fast as you can. I'll meet you there!"

I see her nod and pick up the remote so I turn and dive for the house. I waste precious seconds wrestling with the half hanging screen door before I finally yank it away from the frame and fly into the house. It's like déjà vu when I get part way through the kitchen and see another man fill the front door. I freeze in place like a scared deer when his nasty chuckle rumbles out of him. He only says one word, "Indigo" but it's enough to make me start backing up. As he steps into my home, a glow slowly fills the hallway until Abuela steps between us. She looks my way briefly before glancing at the front door where Boyd has paused. Everything seems to slow right down after that. She leans over and places the lantern she's carrying in one hand and the basket in her other onto the floor. Her foot pushes the basket down the hallway towards me and then swings back to kick the lantern towards Boyd. My mouth gapes open as I watch it arc into the air and then smash into the wall beside the front door. Hot flaming oil splashes in every direction, instantly causing flames to devour the old dry wood of the walls and door frame.

Boyd roars in rage and maybe pain, but I take no satisfaction from it as I watch my home begin to burn. I pull my eyes away from the flames and focus on Abuela. I'm shocked to see her smiling at me as she starts in my direction. Her hand has flipped open the messenger bag she's worn since this morning and just as she pulls something from it, there's an incredibly loud bang. I'm too far away to catch her when she's shoved towards me and then drops to the floor but the object she had removed from her bag slides all the way to a stop at my feet. I can't help but reach down to pick it up. The smooth worn handle of the revolver fits perfectly in my hand and I raise it towards the front door by instinct and pull the trigger. I hear his howl of pain and see him disappear out of sight so I take my chance and rush towards Abuela.

She's gasping for breath on her stomach and trying to pull the strap of the bag over her head when I reach her. I take in the spreading stain of blood on her back before gently turning her over. When her eyes focus on mine, the pain washes away from her face and a beautiful smile emerges. She grips my hand tightly and moves it to the strap she's been fighting with so I lift it over her head.

"The maps, bullets and my Lucas's letters. Take them and run, Día."

I shake my head in despair. "No, Abuela. You are coming with us. I can't do it alone. I need you!" My voice cracks in pain on the last word but I can see she's no longer with me. I suck in a sob and end up choking on a lung full of smoke. I force my eyes to leave her empty ones and look towards the front door. I see it's completely engulfed in flames and they are rushing down the hall towards me. If I stay, I will burn so I bend over and kiss her head once and throw the strap of the bag over my head before pushing to my feet and racing for the back door. I reach down and scoop up the basket she kicked my way on the run. I will not surrender this last bit of love she made for us.

I crash out of the back door with her gun leading the way. If Boyd or any of his thugs are waiting for me I will keep pulling the trigger until either they're all dead or I am. The backyard is empty but it's almost too dark to see so I run for the gate while swiveling my head around to look for danger. I take the time to close the gate quietly in the hopes of buying us a few more moments to escape. We might get lucky if they don't discover it at all in the dark.

My throat is on fire from inhaling the smoke and each breath burns all the way down but I stagger on down the ditch and up the other side, clawing my way up as I go. I hurl myself around the corner of the building and almost run straight into the side of the trailer with the sled covering it as it moves past me towards the main tracks. Confusion has me standing stock still as I try and process how Gloria is moving the train all by herself but I remember in a split second that Beck was with her. An enraged growl escapes from between my clenched teeth and I lunge towards the cart, catching the handle beside the door to pull myself up and into it. With a quick glance, I see him pumping the handle as hard as he can and then I look past him and see Gloria's tear streaked face looking up at me from the bench. My hand is shaking as I raise the gun towards him. I try and order him off but all that comes out is a choked coughing fit that has me sinking to my knees. He looks down at me with an apologetic expression and then quickly looks away and pumps even harder.

His brother just killed the only real mother I've ever had. I want to shoot him dead. I want to order him off the cart. Instead, I turn away from him and Gloria and look back towards our home. The flames are reaching high into the sky as the fire devours my home.

We are moving away from it towards safety, maybe. I know I'm in no condition to pump the handles to keep us moving and we have to put as much distance between us and Boyd as possible. As I turn away from the disappearing life I had, I say nothing to Beck as he pumps away. I drop the rest of the way to the wooden floor, lay my head down on it and close my eyes. I can always shoot him in the morning.

Chapter Nine

Boyd Baker walks around the still smoldering wreckage of the home he had hoped would provide him and his men with a decent amount of food and water. Having Claudia would have been an extra bonus. He fumes silently as he watches some of his men pick through the ashes but there's nothing left to scavenge. He should have noticed sooner that girl was better fed than most of the people left in the town but he hasn't seen her in months. He wanders over to a wooden platform with a hand pump in the middle and gives it a few pumps. When nothing but the thinnest dribble of water comes out he walks away in disgust. Gone, any water or food they had been hiding was now gone. Speaking of gone - he turns his head and sees Marco making his way towards him.

"Well?"

Marco shakes his head. "Sorry, Boyd. No one's seen him since last night. Pete saw him leave the house right before we headed out to come here but he did see which way he went. You think he left town?"

Boyd smirks and turns his head to scan the yard hoping for a hidden patch of garden, but all he sees is dead grass and sand.

"Oh, I think he left. But I don't think he left alone. Beck used to be real sweet on that Claudia girl. I think he made his move on her before I could."

He starts to turn away from the yard when he sees a break in the back hedge. He heads that way thinking he should see where it leads before they move on to the next house they plan on visiting. When he gets close enough to see that there's a gate, he turns and waves a few of his men to follow. Boyd sees the old building as soon as he goes through the gate and starts to grin. Maybe, just maybe, his little brother and the girl didn't go very far after all. The three men move quietly across the field and over the ditch before splitting up to go around the building. Boyd pulls his gun from the waist of his pants and readies himself at the corner before peeking around. When he sees his man on the other corner, he nods once and they both move quickly to the open doors, guns raised. With a glance, he sees that it's empty so he drops his gun arm down and curses.

"Where the HELL did they go?"

He spins to leave when the sun catches a shiny object on the ground. He leans over for a closer look and grunts in disappointment. It's just the old railroad tracks. He takes a few steps back towards the house when he stops at a thought. Why are the tracks shiny? They should be covered in sand and dust like everything else. He spins around and strides back to the tracks but this time follows them towards the main line. Half way there he's rewarded with another clue. A glob of black oil is slowly dissolving into the sand as the sun heats it. Boyd moves past it until he comes to where the siding track splits. The junction going west is dull and can barely be seen under the drifting sand and dust but the one going west is exposed steel like something cleaned it.

Boyd climbs the rest of the way up the slight incline to the main tracks and faces east. What's out there besides the desert wastes? Where could they be going and what are they traveling in? He reaches up and rubs at the oil burn on the side of his face, causing the bullet wound in his arm to flare up. A scowl crosses his face. The old woman who burned him might be dead but the girl shot him and his brother betrayed him. That was two offenses he couldn't overlook. Boyd spins back to the building where his men are waiting and barks down to them, "I need a map!"

Chapter Ten

"I swear, I don't know where they went!" Silvia sobs before her head slams to the side from another blow.

Boyd Baker stares at the scene taking place in the trashed kitchen with increasing anger. He finally has enough and steps forward with a wave of his hand to back his man off before he can hit the sobbing woman again.

"Clearly this isn't working so let's try a different line of questions. Where do you *think* she would go? Who does she know that she could run to?"

Silvia raises a hand to her throbbing cheek and cups it before answering.

"Her Mom, Monica maybe? I don't even know where she is. Bonita never said. Just that she had gone north to try and find her father's people."

Boyd shakes his head. "No, they didn't go north so who else is there? What about her father? Where's he at?"

Silvia shakes her head in panic that she doesn't have the answers this cruel man wants. "He's just some guy Monica hooked up with. He's never been in their lives."

Boyd throws up his hands. "Fine! What about her grandmother's people?"

Silvia heaves in a shaky breath and shakes her head. "Bonita's family were all from Mexico. They disowned her when she married Lucas. They didn't approve of her marrying a white man."

Boyd kicks a table chair across the room to crash into the wall.

"East! They went east! What reason would she have to go east?" He bellows, just inches from Silvia's face. When she just shakes her head frantically that she doesn't know, he shoves away from the table and turns to one of his men. "Go get one of the kids!"

Silvia screams out, "No. No, please! Wait, just wait! I'm trying to think. Please don't hurt my kids!"

Boyd stares down at her in annoyance. "If you don't want me to have a little chat with one of your brats, I suggest you think real hard about what I want to know!"

She holds up her hands and takes a few deep breaths. "Mr. Lucas worked in the east when he was still alive. I don't know where exactly but I'm pretty sure it was out of state."

Boyd stares down at her in thought before pulling a chair around and straddling it backward.

"I'm listening. Tell me about this grandfather. What did he do for work?"

Silvia tries to calm her breathing as she wracks her brain for memories long forgotten then nods at Boyd.

"Ok, he was a prospector. He had some claims in Arizona, I think. He must have done well because they were a wealthy family when I was a child. My mother worked for Bonita as a maid and baby nurse when Monica and I were little. He would be around for a few weeks at a time and then leave again for his claims. I remember one time we all stood by the tracks waving goodbye when he left in his little train car. He always went east until he died out there. That's all I know!"

Boyd leans forward when she mentions the tracks and train. "A train? He had a train? No, we would have heard a train leaving last night!"

At his angry look, she shakes her head. "No! No, it wasn't a train like in the books. It was just a little car that sat on the tracks. There was no engine to make it go. Miss Bonita told me Mr. Lucas would pump a handle to make it move. I remember I was disappointed there was no train whistle."

Boyd leans back and rubs his mouth in thought before glancing over at one of his men with raised eyebrows.

Marco shrugs and says, "I don't know. Maybe a handcart?"

As soon as he said the word handcart, an image of two men see-sawing a handle to move a small platform with wheels down a track fills Boyd's head. He nods at Marco and looks back at Silvia.

"Alright, but where were they going?" When she just shook her head, he stands up and pushes the chair away. "One last question. What did the grandfather prospect for?"

Silvia hesitates for a beat, praying for forgiveness. She knew this man would go after the children and hunt them if she said the one thing he wouldn't be able to resist. The sounds of her kids crying in the next room firmed her resolve and pushed away the guilt before answering.

"Gold."

As the light of greed fills Boyd's eyes and a grin spreads across his face, Silvia looks away in shame. She tries to console herself that he has no way to go after them and he would never be able to survive the desert on foot. A commotion at the front door has those thoughts proved wrong. With much shoving and swearing, Silvia's husband Juan is pushed into the kitchen and onto his knees.

Boyd looks him over with contempt and nods to Peter, the man who brought him in.

"What's this all about?"

Peter gives Juan's head a shove. "It's the husband. He says he came to take his family back to the ranch he's been working at." An ugly laugh rolls out of him. "Says it's not safe here anymore!"

Boyd waves his hand dismissively and starts to turn away but Peter's next words have him turning back in interest.

"This guy's got wheels! He drove right up in a weird looking car."

Boyd looks Juan over with a frown. "How'd you get a car to work? There hasn't been any gas around here for years."

Juan glares up at Boyd and stays stubbornly silent until Boyd walks over and wrenches Silvia's head back with a handful of her hair.

"I can add a few more colors to her face if you'd like or we can bring one of your kids in."

Juan takes in the bruised and swelling face of his wife before he slumps in defeat and shakes his head.

"It doesn't run on gas. It's solar powered and it's not a car. It's a dune buggy."

Boyd releases Silvia and walks back over to Juan. "See, that wasn't so hard. Now, where did you get it? Did you steal it?"

Juan shakes his head. "I don't steal! El patrón of the ranch I've been working at lent it to me to bring my family back. He's letting all the workers bring their families back. The government won't be giving rations or water out anymore so to keep his workers he offered them and their families sanctuary."

Boyd laughs. "What an idiot! All those extra mouths to feed?"

Juan's expression turns to one of contempt. "He's a good man! It's smart business too. His operation is the last major ranch left in this state so if all his workers leave to try and help their families find food and water, the ranch will be done for. This way he takes care of both his workers and his ranch."

Boyd shrugs indifferently. "Whatever. I guess it's lucky for you that you have a place to go. I just hope for your kids' sake it's not that far to walk!" He waves Peter off. "Let him go. We're done here."

As the gang files out of the house, Boyd turns to Marco with a grin. "How much gold do you think we'd need to buy passage over the wall?"

Marco stands beside him on the top step looking down on the rest of the men who are checking out the strange looking vehicle in the street. He lowers his voice so only Boyd can hear him.

"That depends on how many you want to take with you." He turns to him with a shrewd look. "You'd also want as much as possible left once you're over the wall to set up for a new life."

Boyd studies his man with consideration before turning away with a slow nod then goes down the steps to the yard and calls all the men over. Once they have gathered around him, he speaks.

"Alright, listen up! Marco, Peter and I will be taking this dune buggy and going after the girl and my coward of a brother for a little payback. The rest of you need to continue stripping this town of all the food and water you can find. Stock pile it up at the house. We're going to need it. When we get back, we're leaving this deathtrap and headed north!"

Most of the men cheer at this but a few of the smarter ones look unconvinced. One of them steps forward and asks, "Why do you need to waste time going after them? They'll just end up dead out there anyway. If we're going north, then we should just clear this town and go."

Boyd scowls and snarls at him. "I'm the leader of this gang! You don't get to question me!"

A few more of his men frown at the non-answer and step forward so Boyd lets out an annoyed sigh.

"Fine! One, that little brat shot me and my brother betrayed me. They need to answer for that by my hand. Two, they have something that will pave our way to a new life up north. I'm going to get it for all of us. Three, anyone who has an issue with my decision can just stay here and starve to death! Anyone got a problem with that?"

His explanation seems to appease most of them so he waves his hands to get them moving. Once they're out of earshot, he turns to Marco.

"I think three passes over the wall will do." When Marco smiles and nods his agreement, he continues. "Good, let's get loaded up. We need to catch up to those kids. They're the ticket to us finding some gold!"

Chapter Eleven

*E*xcerpt from a private letter.

February 12, 2028

My dearest Bonita,

How I miss you and wish I was home in your warm embrace. Things have gone well here and our claim is playing out richly! I believe we will have more than enough to secure a comfortable future for many years to come.

I wish you had come with me on this trip as I've discovered the most amazing place. I decided to take a break after ten hard days of work and went exploring deeper into the mountains. You know from previous trips with me just how barren and dry this area is so you would have been just as shocked as I was to stumble into a lush green valley in the middle of this desolate land. A brilliant blue stream, the color of your eyes, runs down the middle of it with green grasses and wildflowers covering both banks. The stream is fed by a twenty-foot waterfall that pours from an opening in the valley wall with a large pool at its base. I swear, I thought I was sun-touched and delirious so I sat for a good hour just gazing down at the beauty of it before I convinced myself it was real.

I made my way down and had to laugh as I startled a small herd of mule deer from where they had been drinking at the stream. When I reached the pool at the bottom of the waterfall, I stripped down to my birthday suit and dove right in. The cool water was crystal clear and tasted as sweet as wine. How I wished you were there with me to enjoy that moment.

I laid down in the soft grass of the meadow beside the stream and let the sun dry my body as I planned how I would build a beautiful home for you right where I was laying. It will be the perfect location for us to escape the troubles that our nation is going through. A safe haven where we can raise and grow our family. I know you will love it as much as I do.

I can't wait to be home with you and plan to leave soon. I'm including a few pictures of the valley that I've scanned in so you can see why I'm so excited by it. I truly haven't seen such lush natural vegetation since I left British Columbia. You know how much I love our life in California but seeing this valley gave me a powerful longing for the green landscape of my childhood.

I hope this data file reaches you today and the mail satellites aren't backed up again!

All my love for you.

Your adoring husband,

Lucas

The first thing I notice when I wake up is that Glo has curled up against me. The next thing I notice is that we're not in bed but on a hard wooden floor. The confusion only lasts for a second when the memories of what happened to Abuela and our home come flooding back. When I remember Beck pumping the handle to get us away from his brother, I shove myself to my feet and frantically look around the cart to find him. The breath and tension whoosh out of me when I see him sleeping at the other end of the cart. I study his peaceful face as he sleeps and I try to see the boy I once knew in the man he's almost become. The only thing that looks the same to me is his brown wavy hair that has golden highlights running through it.

I shake my head. It doesn't matter what he looks like. I need to decide if he's a threat to my sister and me. I know he's been in his brother's gang but everything I've seen from him in the last twenty-four hours says he's not like the rest of them. He let us pass after the ration station when his brother's men would have robbed us of our supplies. And if he was a threat to us, then why did he not only race to warn us about the attack that was coming but flee from his brother with us too? I don't know the answers to these questions but I do know that I don't trust him. As far I can tell, he came to our house empty handed so he could be after our food and water. I pat the messenger bag that's still over my shoulder. The old gun that's inside it will be our safety net if he tries anything.

I'm surprised and take a step back when his eyes suddenly fly open and he launches to his feet. His moves are so sudden that I'm clawing open the bag to get to the gun but pause when he spins away from me and rushes to the windows. He moves from each one scanning the desert in all directions before slumping down on the padded bench with a deep sigh. His eyes lift to mine and I'm surprised to see that they're full of weariness. His voice is a dry croak when he speaks.

"I'm sorry I fell asleep. I just couldn't pump anymore and I was worried there might be something on the tracks I wouldn't see in the dark."

I just stare at him in silence trying to figure him out. He's sorry he had to rest and he was trying to keep us from having an accident in the dark? I don't get how he can be robbing people one day and trying to be a hero the next so I just give him a curt nod and turn away. I walk around the center handles and pull two jugs of water from the shelves before returning and handing him one. I watch him as we both drink deeply and try not to wince at the stale plastic taste of the water. It's better than the taste of smoke and ash that I woke with.

When he finishes drinking he turns and looks back out of a window with a frown then says over his shoulder, "We should do our business and get going. I don't know how far we got last night so we might not have much of a lead on him."

I take another step back from him but this time it's in disbelief. "What are you talking about? What lead? You can't seriously think he's going to come after us, do you?"

He turns all the way around to face me with a grim expression. "You don't know Boyd like I do. He'll come for us. Even if it's just to save face with his men."

I shake my head. "How? Does he have transportation? He'd die out here on foot!"

Beck huffs out a breath. "It doesn't matter. He'll find a way. We should go…soon."

I chew on my bottom lip in worry for a few seconds before a dark thought swims into my head. "Is he coming for me or is he coming for you? Cause if it's you he's after then you can get off right now. I'm not going to let you put my sister in danger!" I practically spit at him.

I expect a reaction from him but all I get is sad eyes that look beyond tired. "It's both of us. You defied him by running when he wanted you and what supplies you have and I betrayed him by warning you and then leaving with you. He's going to want revenge, so like I said, we should go and put as many miles between us and him as possible."

I want to argue that he wouldn't care about me, but if he's that deranged, then me shooting at him probably sealed my fate. Before I can say anything else, Gloria's voice pipes in.

"Día, I have to go."

I whirl around to see her staring at me with big scared eyes while she shuffles back and forth in need. I can tell she's ready to burst and also that she's overheard what Beck's said about his brother coming after us. I nod to her and turn to Beck.

"You get off first and then wait for us before you get back on." I don't want to chance him taking off on us. I see by his expression that he understands my meaning but he only nods slowly and pushes off the bench. I watch him climb down the steps and move around to the other side of the tracks so I hop down and turn to lift Glo down. We don't go far to do our morning business and then I rush her back to the cart. As soon as Beck hears us open the door, he comes around and stares at me before looking back towards our home.

"I'm not a threat to you. All I ever wanted was a way to get away from my brother. I didn't warn you because I wanted something. I did it because it was the right thing to do and we used to be friends. You can leave me here if you think you'd be better off without me but I think it would be a mistake. I can help with the pumping and if Boyd does find us, I'll fight him. I'm done being his punching bag!"

I look up at Gloria who's standing in the doorway. I don't know if I'm strong enough to protect her. I don't know what we'll find down the tracks. Having Beck with us might make all the difference in our survival. I turn from her worried face to his.

"You don't even know where we're going!"

He shakes his head and I see a small smile start to form on his face.

"I don't even care. All that matters to me is that it's away from Boyd and...I'm not alone anymore." He blushes and looks away so I glance back at Gloria. She meets my eyes and gives a firm nod so I turn back to Beck and point at the door.

"Start pumping!"

He won't meet my eyes when he nods but I can see the relief in his expression as he moves towards the steps. I go up ahead of him and start rummaging around in the basket that Abuela slid to me last night. It's filled with prepared food that will see us through the next few days. I pass a wrapped tortilla that's filled with sprouts and peppers to Glo and take one for myself. I catch Beck's glance as he starts pumping the handle and then hold the wrap up to him.

"There's one here for you too. Just let me get this down and I'll take over so you can eat."

He gives me a small smile of gratitude before focusing ahead out the front windows. I'm about to take a bite of my breakfast when I feel a tug on my sleeve. I turn to Glo and see the sadness and uncertainty in her eyes.

"What happened? Where's Abuela?"

I take that bite of food to stall for time and look out at the slowly passing desert. The sun is just starting to rise on a new day. A day that will change Gloria's life forever. I try and think of the words to explain to her that her home and the only mother she's ever known is gone for good but the food sticks in my throat with the grief that washes over me. When she tugs at my sleeve again, I grab the jug of water and wash down the sticky mess.

"A gang came to the house to steal everything. They had a gun. Abuela…she…she saved me, us. She gave her life so we could get away."

Gloria looks down at the wrap in her hand with a frown then back to me. "Will she be following us? Is she going to meet up with us later?"

I swallow hard and briefly close my eyes, hating to say the words but knowing I have to tell her so she'll understand. "I'm sorry, Glo. She…she died."

Gloria sucks in a breath at the words and I see tears spring into her eyes. "But, where are we going then?"

I shoot a look over at Beck but his eyes stay fixed ahead. Even so, I can see the shame that he's feeling. I want to be angry at him. Rage at him for what his brother has done but all I feel is sadness so I turn back to her.

"We're going to a better place. A place Abuela wanted us to go to. It's very far away and it will be a hard journey but it will be worth it."

Her little chin trembles as she nods her head but I can't think of anything else to say to her to make this better. I let her go as she takes her wrap and moves to the far end of the bench to watch out the front windows. I look down at my own wrap but my appetite is gone and once again the taste of smoke and ash fills the back of my throat. I shake my head to try and get the image of Abuela surrounded by flames out of my mind but it doesn't work. Instead, I wrap my food back up into the paper and cloth it was packed in and stand up, motioning Beck to trade spots with me. I need some mindless physical action to clear my head. I pump in silence as I try and do the math of how far we need to go. Abuela just said hundreds of miles. I don't know if that means two hundred or eight hundred. I'll have to look over the maps in the messenger bag when I trade back with Beck. I remember her talking about three junctions and to take the third so I call out to Glo.

"I need you to watch the tracks for anything on them so we have time to stop. Also, watch closely for the tracks to split off in a different direction! We must take the third junction. It's very important we don't miss it!"

She doesn't turn back to me but I see her head nod so I leave her be. Grief is a beast that sometimes needs to be faced alone. With Glo watching the tracks for me, I put my head down and lose myself in the rhythmic pumping, every now and then raising my eyes to the gauge that shows our speed. I find the easiest speed for me to maintain is between ten and twelve miles an hour. I try and calculate how far we can go in how many days before our water runs out at this speed. I need to look at the rail map for the exact distance to do the calculations. If we run out of water before we get to the place called Coyote Rock, we won't have any for the part of the journey we have to go on foot. All the pumping in the world won't matter then. We'll be in the middle of the desert and dead.

Chapter Twelve

Boyd Baker grits his teeth against the nausea sloshing around in his stomach. He refuses to let his men know how sick and fearful he is of riding in this death machine. He had waved Marco into the driver's seat once they were ready to go because he didn't have the first idea of how to work the vehicle and he didn't want the two men laughing at him. It was clear from the start that Marco was just as clueless causing the machine to lurch ahead and slam to a stop. Once he got the hang of it though, they had picked up speed and the motion was causing Boyd to feel sick and scared. He had never ridden in anything that moved before and even the twenty-five miles an hour speed was terrifying to him.

Marco swerved sharply to avoid a clump of sage brush, sending Boyd flying hard into the passenger door and the contents of his stomach into his throat. They were driving beside the old railroad tracks on the hard-packed sands that the oversized tires handled well. The hot sun was high in the sky so Boyd assumed it was around noon. They had started hitting houses first thing in the morning and had cleaned out quite a few when one of his men remembered that Silvia was a friend to Claudia's family. The information he had gotten out of her was going to change his life. The way he figured it, the girl had only one reason to head east deeper into the desert and that was to get the gold her grandfather had mined. It was the only thing that would give her and her sister a shot at a new life somewhere else. There was nowhere else to the east for her to go. All the major cities were death traps filled with gangs and bandits that had crossed over from Mexico when the government had abandoned the lower states. She wouldn't risk taking a small child into any of them so it had to be the gold she was after.

As the hot sun burned down on him, he dreamed about what it would be like to have enough gold for passage over the wall. He had heard whispers and soft-spoken rumors of cool weather and endless lakes of water. Not one day of his life had he felt anything but hot, sticky, and sweaty. He planned to change all that. He deserved more than this dry, dusty heat-scape and he was going to get it no matter who stood in his way.

He figured the girl and his coward of a brother had an eighteen-hour lead on him but they would only be traveling at half the speed of the dune buggy so they should catch up to them in under a day. Just then, the wheels on his side hit a half-buried rock sending him flying into the air only to slam his head against the roll bar. He dropped back down half into his seat and then forward causing his arm and face to slam into the hard-plastic dash when Marco slammed on the brakes. The wounds on his arm and face screamed out in pain from the contact making him let out a roar of rage. He was ready to call this journey a wash and return to town when the burning fire of vengeance reared its ugly head, reminding him of how he was wounded in the first place.

He sat fuming while Pete reached around him from the back seat and pulled a belt across his lap and buckled him in. He would find them and when he did he would make them pay, in so many ways!

Chapter Thirteen

I pump for what feels like hours but judging from the height of the sun it's only around noon. The small cart's insufferable with heat and my shoulders and arms burn in pain like they never have before. The sweat dripping down my face stings my eyes and when I turn my head to rub it against the already sweat damp shoulder of my shirt, I see a flash of green. At first I don't know what it means. My eyes are blurry from the sweat that's dripped into them so I can't make out the words on the label under the green light so I step away from the handle and lean closer. The words come clear for my tired eyes and I let out a groan of relief. "Engine charged" might be the sweetest words on earth right now. My arm's wobbly with exhaustion when I reach out and stab the button but I'm smiling as I feel the cart pick up speed that didn't come from my pumping.

"Whoa! What's happening?" Beck asks in concern.

I turn to him and breathe the words out. "The engine is charged. No more pumping for a few hours."

"There's an engine?" he asks.

I just nod and turn to the closest window. Now that I'm not pumping my mind can focus on the next problem. It's so hot in the car that we've all been guzzling water like crazy. If we keep going at the rate of the last few hours then we won't make it more than a few days before we're out. There has to be a way to get air moving to cool the inside and us down. I run my hands around the frame of the window looking for a latch of some kind but all I find is two raised metal stubs on either side of the top of the frame that move towards the middle of the window but every time I push one it just bounces back without doing anything.

I feel Beck move behind me and his arms come around me on both sides causing me to tense and get ready to slam my elbow back into his stomach as hard as I can. What does he think he's doing getting in my personal space? I brace myself to swing back when I see the window drop down an inch and my mouth drops open.

"You have to squeeze them together at the same time for it to lower." He says against the side of my ear. His breath feels cool against my sweat dampened hair and a pleasant shiver runs down my spine, causing me to elbow him away anyway, just not as hard as I had originally planned. I tuck my lips in together to stop the smile that wants to form when I hear him let out an "oomph" from the blow and feel him back off.

I reach up and squeeze the springs together like he said and glide the window down as far as it will go. When I turn around and see the hurt frown on his face, I shrug.

"Thanks for the help. I just don't like anyone in my space. Can you do that side of the cart?"

He gives me a disgruntled nod and rolls his eyes but I can see the small spark of humor in them so I just turn away and work on opening all the windows on my side of the cart. When I get to the front, I stand for a moment behind Glo and search for words to comfort her. Other than drinking from the jug, she hasn't moved from her spot at the front window since this morning. At a loss for words, I finally just reach around her and pull her gently back against me. She stays stiff for a moment but then lets herself melt back into me.

We stay like that for a few minutes before I turn her around to face me.

"I have some things from Abuela that I'd like to share with you but first we need to make some decisions about…" I nod my head back towards our stowaway.

A tiny grin forms on her lips and she leans to the side to peek past me at him before ducking back.

"I like him! He's really nice and it's fun to have a boy around."

I snort out a laugh at that. Living in a house of females has shielded her from all the annoying traits of "boys". But she is right, he does seem to be nice so far and I have to admit, this whole crazy journey seems more manageable with another semi adult to share the load. I let out a sigh and muss up her hair.

"Well, let's go see what the boy has to say for himself!"

She smiles but shakes her head. "You go. I have to watch the tracks so we don't hit anything and I'm still watching for them to split like you said."

I lean down and plant a smacking kiss on the top of her head. "I knew I could count on you! I'll take over in a little while so you can rest your eyes." She bobs her head and spins around to go back to her watch.

I turn to talk to Beck about his plans but the words catch in my throat when I see him with his head stuck out one of the windows. His eyes are closed against the wind our increased speed has created and I try not to laugh at the way his shaggy hair is whipping all around. It's then that I realize that the temperature in the cart has dropped. It's not cool by any means but it's definitely more bearable than the hot box it was. I take a few steps towards him and give a yank on his shirt to bring him back inside. When his head pops back in, the grin on his face is one I recognized from our childhood. It's the first time I see my old friend in him.

"This is amazing! We're going so fast! I've never been in anything that moves with this kind of speed before. Can you imagine what it must have been like back when there were cars and trucks that went even faster? Or the sky trains? I read about them in a book once. That would be so incredible to fly through the air like that!"

I just stand there with a dumb grin on my face as memories of this boy come flashing back to me. I always loved how excited he would get about the things he would read about in his books. He would jabber at me constantly about technical marvels or faraway places with strange names, foods, and customs. He always said we would travel to those places when we grew up. And here we are, my old friend and I running away from home together.

"What? Why are you looking at me like that?" he asks, as the excitement dims from his face.

I just shake my head. "Hi Beck, it's good to see you again."

His face fills with sadness and his eyes cast down to the floor. "Día, I'm sorry. Boyd would have found a way to hurt you. It was his mission in life to take everything good away from me. I didn't want to see you hurt so when he shoved you that day, I had to stop being your friend for your own protection." His eyes lift to meet mine. "It sucked not having you as my friend all these years. I missed you."

I feel a sting of tears at the back of my eyes. The truth is, I missed him too. I never really had anyone to talk to after that day. As much as I loved Glo and Abuela, sometimes you just need a friend. I clear my throat and shove the feelings of loneliness away. I need to think about the here and now. The bottom line is, he's not my friend now and I don't know if I can trust him yet.

"We need to talk about where you're going."

He gives me a confused look. "What do you mean?"

"I mean, when and where you're going to get off this cart."

Chapter Fourteen

I ignore the hurt that floods into his eyes and take a seat on the bench so I can put the messenger bag on my lap. I open it up and thumb through the envelopes and other papers in it until I come to the rail map. I pull it out and unfold it until I can find our town and then fold it back up into a manageable size. My eyes lift to his and I nod my head to the bench beside me. He sits slowly but doesn't say anything to answer my question so I put half the map on both our laps and point to our town.

"This is where we started. There are three junctions ahead of us you can choose from that lead to what used to be major cities. There will be people in them and a chance for you to start over somewhere new."

He leans over the map and studies it before asking in a small voice, "Which one are you guys going to?"

I shake my head and try to ignore the guilt his tone makes me feel. "None of them."

He leans away from the map and looks at me but I keep my gaze down like I'm still studying the map.

"You have somewhere to go? You have a destination in mind?" he asks.

I nod again and then bite my lip when he asks in that same small voice, "Can't I come with you guys?"

I finally lift my eyes to meet his and wish I hadn't.

"Why?" I choke out when I see the desperate loneliness in them. "Why do you want to come with us? You could go anywhere. Be anyone. Start fresh."

He turns his head away and I see his jaw tighten. My questions hang in the air between us for a good five minutes before all the air leaves his lungs in a rush. When he turns to me there are tears welled up in his eyes but his expression is angry.

"I'm tired. I'm tired of being alone. I have no family that cares for me, no friends, and now I have no home! The only friend I ever had was you so is it so hard for you to understand that I don't want to go anywhere or be anyone all by myself? I just don't want to be alone anymore! If you really hate me that much then close your eyes and pick a spot on the map and that's where I'll get off!"

I can feel my jaw hanging open at his tirade. I'm at a loss for words at the sheer amount of pain this boy is living with. I have no idea how to respond but the decision is taken out of my hands when a small hand reaches past me and rests against his cheek.

"We don't have a home anymore either and our family died yesterday. We don't have to be alone. We can be a family together. Día and I would love if you came with us Beck."

When I see a lone tear break free and run down his face, I know I'm lost. This broken boy will be coming with us. I swallow down the shame I feel for adding to his pain and clear my throat.

"Well, I guess I should tell you both where we're going then."

Glo hops up and down and yells, "Yay!" while Beck works at getting his composure back with a tentative, grateful nod.

I pull out the faded pictures and lay them on top of the map. "This is my Grandfather's secret garden. He was a prospector in the Mohave's Black Mountains in Arizona. He found it hidden away on one of his trips and built a house there for Abuela and him to live in.

She didn't want to live in a place so far away and isolated with a small baby so no one but him has ever been there. There is a natural spring that feeds a tall waterfall that created a small pool and stream that flows through the valley. She said that you can grow crops there and that there are lots of wildlife to hunt for meat." I look at them both and sigh. "I don't know if it's there. All I have to go on is what she said, these three pictures and an old map. We could be going to our deaths if it's not there but I don't have any other ideas on where to go."

Glo picks up the picture of the waterfall and studies it closely. "I've never seen this much water in one place before!"

I smile a sad smile. "None of us have, sweetie. We haven't seen a lake, a stream or any type of natural body of water. The only water I've ever seen in my whole life has been what came out of the pump on our well."

She looks up with a beaming smile. "I want to see this, please!"

I take the picture back from her and look at it again. "So do I but we can't know for sure if it's really there. This picture was taken over thirty years ago. That water might be long dried up like the rest. The question is, do we take a chance on our lives that it's still there or try and go somewhere else?"

I glance over at Beck, who hasn't said anything yet, and see him studying the other two pictures. He must feel my eyes on him because he looks up and asks, "Why can't we check it out and if it's gone dry then try for somewhere else?"

I huff out a breath of frustration. "Because we don't have enough water to do that! Once we stop after the third junction, we go overland on foot. We only have what water we brought with us and there's no way for us to get more that I know of. Most or all of it will be gone by the time we find this place. We won't have enough to survive a trip back to the cart and then forward to somewhere else."

His eyes track over to the shelves on the opposite side of the cart and the water jugs stored there. His brow furrows in thought before asking, "Do you know exactly how far we will be traveling?"

I give a shrug. "Not exactly but I think we can work it out with these maps."

He nods his head and moves his finger along the route we are taking before running it back and past where we started to the edge of the country. A slight smile tugs at his lips.

"Wouldn't it be amazing to go to the ocean? To see water with no end?"

I roll my eyes. "Sure, and then die of radiation or worse but hey, we got to see it first, right?"

He looks sheepish when he nods. "I know it's not an option but I wish we could just go there, get on a ship and sail to a new land that's better than here."

I point to a northern spot on the map. "Last thing I remember learning in school about that was all shipping goes here now and it's on the other side of the wall so not an option. And I hate to say it but I don't think there is a better place out there anymore that's not behind a wall. With all the coasts flooded or bombed and the interior nothing but desert and ruins, I think the best we can hope for is a small pocket of land like the valley that we can survive in."

He lets out a defeated sigh. "I know, just dreaming. Anyways, I can start figuring out distances. Any idea how far we've come and how long we have until we have to start pumping again?"

I stand up and check on Glo, who's gone back to the front window before moving over to the control panel and taking a good look at every gauge and button for the first time. I'm surprised and happy to see the speedometer steady at twenty-three miles an hour. That's double the speed we were making when I was pumping. The engine charge light is still in the green with two bars to go before it goes to yellow so I'm guessing we have at least an hour and a half of charge left before it's back to pumping. There's a little glass square with four zeros, an eight and a two that slowly changes to a three as I'm watching it so I guess that it's keeping track of the miles we travel. I think about how far eighty-three miles is from home but I don't really understand just how far that is. All I know is Abuela said we would go hundreds of miles before we stopped.

I go back to Beck and tell him what I learned. His eyebrows jump in surprise at how fast we're going and how far we've gone. His finger shows me on the map but it doesn't look that far to me.

"How long will it take for the engine to charge back up once it runs out of power? If we can keep going this fast, it should only take us three days at most to get to where we stop."

I shrug my shoulders again. "No idea. It's not like this thing came with instructions. We were pumping for around five hours today when the green light came on but this thing had been sitting in a dark building for decades so it might have taken longer than normal for that first charge. Just go with the five hours for now until we know from the next charge."

He nods in agreement and starts adding up numbers. I try not to laugh at him when I see his tongue poke out of his mouth as he does the calculations. He used to do the same thing when we were kids and he was reading something that confused him. I still find it hard to trust him but now that I've shared our destination with him, I don't have a choice.

He catches me looking at him with the amused expression on my face so I quickly lean in and tap the map asking, "Well?"

He gives me a look but just tells me his figures.

"So, it looks like we have a total of four hundred and thirty miles to get to our stop. If the engine goes for two hours a day for fifty miles and we pump eighty miles that takes us one hundred and thirty miles a day. That's roughly three and a half days but say four just to be on the safe side. How much water do we have?"

I glance at the jugs on the shelves and then nudge the two half empty ones on the floor at our feet before answering.

"We started with twenty. These two halves make nineteen left."

He starts counting on his fingers and then bites his lip in thought.

"Ok, if we stick to no more than two jugs a day that gives us ten days of water. Let's say it takes us two days on foot to get to the valley so we'll use up twelve of the jugs getting there leaving us eight in reserve." He looks back down on the map and taps on a blue squiggly line that we will be crossing close to the end of our rail journey. "This used to be a huge river. It was the main water source for this region of the country. We learned in school about it. Do you remember?"

I think back on what we were taught about the water wars and remember that the drying up of this river was the start of the conflicts so I nod and he continues.

"There might still be a little water here. Not enough to support all the population that used to live here but enough that we might be able to refill some of the empty jugs when we get there. If not, we still have the eight jugs if the valley is dry and we need to come back to the cart. That will give us enough to get back and try for somewhere else."

I feel my shoulders tense at the thought of a dry valley. Sure, we'd have enough water to get back to the cart and continue on for a few days but the problem is, where? Where are we supposed to go that we can survive? I look away from him and down to the map with all the lines that seem to go nowhere. That's exactly it, there is nowhere for us to go.

Chapter Fifteen

We pass the first junction not too long after that with Glo yelling out in excitement as she spots it. I tell her how good a job she's doing and she beams with pride. I'm so thankful she's such an easy-going girl and it takes so little to bring her happiness. After that, we all sit lost in our thoughts as mile after mile of empty desert passes by. I find my eyes constantly drawn back to the power gauge as it drops bar by bar into the yellow and then finally into the red. When there are only two red bars left, we all feel the change in speed. I go to push myself to my feet but Beck beats me to it and takes his place at the handle. I give him a grateful smile as I pass around him to switch the button on the control panel under the meter over to charge.

With the sun at its hottest point of the day and the reduced speed, the cart starts heating up again. It's not quite as bad as it was this morning with all the windows closed up but it's very uncomfortable for all of us. At home, we would be hiding indoors with all the windows covered during this part of the day but out here in the open, we have no choice but to bear the heat. With nothing to distract us but the endless sand and scrub outside, I try and take our minds off of it by reading my Grandfather's letters out loud.

Excerpt from a private letter.

My Darling Bonita,

Things have gone well on our claims and both of the veins are still producing out nicely. A few more trips out here and we will never want for anything again. I know my trips away have become longer than they used to but there is a reason for that. I'm very concerned with the way the war is going and I'm afraid the south will lose. If that happens, we will be forced out of our home. I hate the idea of returning to the north. We both know all the reasons I left there in the first place so, with that in mind, I have a huge surprise for you!

I'm writing you from our secret valley that is as beautiful and as lush as ever. I have spent much of the time away from you working on our claims but also hauling in supplies to the valley. I have begun construction on a home for us. It will be a haven for us if we are forced out of California. We will be able to live here in peace and safety with all the water we will ever need. You will laugh at the idea of your miner being a simple farmer but I would gladly give up all the trappings gold brings us if we can be together and safe. At night when it's too dark to work I study up on raising crops and how to preserve them so when the time comes I will be able to grow our food and take care of us.

I'm most excited by the front porch that I will build along the length of our home. I dream of us sitting on it watching the waterfall as the sound of our children's laughter fills the valley. It's a beautiful dream that I can't wait to share with you.

A few more weeks, my love, and I will be home in your arms again for a while.

All my love,

Lucas

I lower the letter onto my lap and let out a sigh. How I wish I could have known my grandfather. He sounds like such a good man who clearly loved his wife very much. What a different life we would have led if he hadn't died so young and been around to see us through the aftermath of the war. Maybe my mother would have turned out different. She might have stuck around and I would have a father whose name I knew. I don't know how my life would be if grandfather had lived but I'm grateful that he put the effort into building a home away from the dangers of our world. If it's still there.

I look out the windows and see the sun is making its descent. There will only be a few hours of light left and then we'll have to stop for the night. So far there hasn't been anything blocking the tracks but we can't take the chance of something damaging the cart. We would never survive on foot out here. I glance over at the power gauge and I'm surprised to see it's already half way back into the yellow. Beck's been pumping for over an hour so I guess I was right that it took longer to charge the first time because it had been sitting in the dark building for so long. If it only takes a couple hours to charge back to full, we'll make way better time than Beck's estimates which also means we'll use up less water and have more in reserve if we have to turn back from the valley. It also means Beck and I will only have to pump for two hours each time to recharge the battery making it less physically challenging for us.

I jump to my feet with that happy thought and wave him away from the handle to take a turn. He slumps away from it and shakes out the pain in his arms. He probably doesn't have the same muscle group developed as I do from all the hand pumping at home. The thought dims my good mood. It reminds me that he's been getting his water all this time from stealing it from the families in town.

He must see something in my expression as I start to pump because he asks me what's wrong. I ignore him and work on getting back into a rhythm but he won't let it go.

"Día, what's wrong? Did I do something?"

I roll my eyes when he asks again and spit out the question that's burning inside me.

"How did you live with yourself?" At his blank expression, I let him have it. "You took water and food from people who were barely getting by as it is. People with children! So how do you live with yourself?"

At first, his face fills with shame but then it morphs into anger and his words come out harshly.

"I wouldn't call the last four years of my life 'living'! I did what I could to run interference so some of the people could get away with at least some of their rations. Other times, I'd sneak away from the house with what I could carry and leave it on the steps or porches of homes that I knew had kids living there. Sometimes I'd get away with it and sometimes Boyd or his men would find out. So you want to know how I live with myself? I lived with a beating at least once a week, sometimes more. That's how I lived. We didn't all get to grow up in a house with food and water and love, Día. Some of us just had to find a way to live period."

His words make me feel my own shame. He's right that I was lucky that Abuela had more to provide for us. I have no right to judge him for something he had no control over and I have no idea what I would be capable of doing to keep Glo alive if we had nothing. I know in my heart I would steal for her to live another day. I try and meet his eyes as I pump to show him my understanding but his back is stiff and firmly facing away from me. I look ahead and see something I never thought I would. Gloria is staring back at me with a frown and eyes that are full of disappointment...of me.

I spend the next hour with my head down pumping out a rhythm that keeps us going at a steady twelve miles an hour. By the end of it, my stomach is growling and complaining about only having the one wrap I ate for breakfast. My knees almost give out when I see the final bar of green light up. I know my hand is shaking as I reach out and push the button so the engine takes over.

The increase of speed has Beck finally looking to me and then over to the power gauge in surprise. His eyes track back to mine but all I get from him is a curt nod before he turns away again so I speak to his back.

"It looks like we only have an hour or so of light left in the day so I figure we can make some good time before we call it for the night."

I see his shoulders shrug but that's it, so I sigh and call out to my sister.

"Hey Glo, you ready to help me make some supper?"

She whips around to face me and makes an exaggerated head nod while holding her stomach like she's in pain.

"I think my tummy's trying to eat itself, it's sooooo hungry!"

It feels good to laugh for a moment but it ends too quickly when she looks at Beck and asks in a soft voice, "Beck, will you watch the tracks for me so I can help make supper?" Her tone is like she's talking to a wounded animal and I know it's my fault but I don't say anything.

I turn away from them both and pull the basket of food off of the shelf. I still haven't looked through the contents of it so I start laying everything out on the bench. There's another set of three filled wraps we can have for breakfast that I set aside. Next comes a bag full of nuts and one with a mix of dried fruit. There's a cloth covering a stack of tortillas and a small pot of Abuela's homemade jam that will make a delicious treat. But for our dinner, I find six baked potatoes and a thermos of homemade soup. Everything is cold but my mouth waters at the thought of the meal. At the bottom of the basket are three old, scratched plastic cups and two shakers of her special herb blend.

Glo holds the cups as I carefully pour the cold soup into them and then watches as I break open the jackets of three of the baked potatoes and sprinkle them with the herbs. Once I'm done, I take a cup of soup and a potato down to where Beck sits and hold them out to him. He stares so long at them that I don't think he'll take them so I swallow hard and say, "I'm sorry Beck. I had no right to judge you. I know you were in an impossible position. I wish there was something I could have done to help you back then."

His eyes finally rise to meet mine and he huffs out a half laugh. "You did try, remember? It got you shoved to the ground. I wasn't willing to let you do anything else. I wasn't willing to see you hurt worse. You have nothing to be sorry about, Día. I'm not mad at you. I'm mad at Boyd, the world and myself. Hopefully, things can be different now." His eyes are full of sadness when he reaches out and takes the food from me with a nod of thanks.

I nod back but don't know what to say so I just return to Glo and settle down to eat. Before I can take my first sip of soup, she's grabbed my hand and bowed her head to say grace. I keep my head up and eyes outside on the passing land but when I hear ask God to watch over Abuela, I find myself bowing my head too as she says the rest of her prayer.

"Thank you for our food and this amazing cart to travel in. Thank you for bringing Beck to us and help him to forgive himself for the bad things he was forced to do. Help us be strong on the journey ahead and please Lord, let there be a waterfall in the valley! Amen!"

I can only marvel at this sweet and kind girl, her eyes sparkling with delight as she stuffs almost half of her potato into her mouth. I shake my head at her and see Beck looking at us from over her head. The sadness is gone from his eyes and has been replaced by gratitude. I know it's for Glo and I also know she's made a fan for life. That's a good thing because I think it will take both of us to see this precious girl through what's ahead.

Chapter Sixteen

Boyd Baker kicks a dent in the door of the dune buggy as he roars out his frustration. After a long day riding in this death machine exposed to the harsh sun, fighting motion sickness the whole way, they still haven't caught up with his prey. Now the machine is dead in the middle of the desert with no charge. He shoves away from it, spins to look out into the wastes and feels the ground sway underneath him as his body works to acclimatize itself to no longer moving.

"Easy there, Boss! We need this thing to get back home. If you bash it too much, we'll be walking back!" Marco cautions.

Boyd spins back to face him with a glare. "Fine! How long until it's ready to move again?" He asks through gritted teeth.

Marco shoots a nervous glance at Pete before answering. "Uh, we had it pegged at full speed for most of the trip so we used the entire charge up. It'll take at least a few hours to power back up." He looks at the lowering sun and hesitantly finishes with, "We're probably done for the day."

Boyd scowls at his men but knows they aren't to blame. His brother and the girl are. They're the reason he's stuck out here. He pushes the burning anger down with a deep breath.

"How far have we come?"

Marco leans into the buggy and checks the odometer. "Looks like one hundred and eighteen miles."

Boyd nods in annoyance. "We should have caught up to them by now! How fast could the two of them be pumping that thing?"

Pete answers this time. "I guess it depends if they went all night. I doubt they would have, too hard on the body to keep that up. They're probably just a few miles further up the track. We'll catch up to them in the morning, Boss."

Boyd looks down the tracks and imagines his prey being that close. He's frustrated but knowing tomorrow will bring his revenge settles him down.

"Alright, if we're stuck here for the night let's get set up. Pete, you put up the tent and Marco, get some food going."

Boyd feels the burning rage creep back up into his throat as he sees the two men exchange nervous looks so he barks at them.

"What's the problem now?"

Marco nods at Pete to speak. "Well, uh, we didn't pack a tent. We thought we would catch up to them real quick and then head back so we only brought food and water."

Boyd's too furious at their incompetence to speak so he just stomps over to the back end of the buggy and starts pulling the bags of food and jugs of water out of the cargo space, dumping them on the ground. Once it's empty he can see a storage compartment so he flips it up and takes an inventory in the day's dying light. There's not much - a tire repair kit, a sealed bag of some type of jerky, four Mylar water pouches, a flare gun with three flare cartridges and an old canvas tarp with a coil of rope wrapped in it. He leaves everything in there except the tarp and rope and drops it at his men's feet.

"Figure it out and get me some food!"

He walks away to the front of the buggy and leans against the hood, staring off into the distance.

"Enjoy your last night of freedom, brother. Tomorrow, you're mine!" He whispers under his breath fiercely. He has no plans on killing his brother. After all, Beck is the only family he has left but there will be a severe lesson delivered that will leave scars as a reminder of who he belongs to for the rest of his miserable life. As for the girl and her brat sister...he isn't one hundred percent certain whether they will make it out of this desert alive. An ugly grin crosses his features. He is sure that after he's done with them, they might not want to live another day!

Chapter Seventeen

When I wake the sun hasn't appeared over the horizon yet and everything has a bluish tint to it. I lay quietly for a moment just thinking about what's to come and everything that's behind us. My heart aches, missing Abuela. It's impossible for me to try and see a future without her there to guide us. Knowing that Glo will have to grow up without her makes it even worse. I'm all she has now. Sister and now mother too. I let my eyes wander down the cart and watch Beck as he sleeps. I've resigned myself to him being with us now but I don't really know how he fits. The memories of my childhood friend clash with what I know of him as a man. He seems sincere about never going back and wanting to be a part of our lives but it's hard not to think of the things he's done to the people of our town, even if he was forced to do those things by his brother. All I really know right now is that I need him. I don't think I'm strong enough to make this journey on my own and protect Glo too. I have to trust him for now but the future is still wide open on whether he will be with us for the long haul.

My bladder's making noises that it needs release so I try and quietly push myself up off the floor without waking the others. The involuntary moan of pain that escapes me from the ache in my arms and shoulders ends that option. I see both Glo and Beck stirring as I make another attempt to stand. Apparently, all those years of pumping the well weren't enough to condition my body for the work

I did yesterday. I don't feel quite so bad about it when I hear Beck's groans mimicking mine. At least I'm not alone in my suffering!

Beck and I shuffle out the door and down the steps while Glo bounces down them. She's got energy to burn from sitting around doing nothing yesterday. After we do our morning business, I stand in the silence of the desert and take a deep breath. It's not cool by any means but the fierce heat is missing from the air. I know that this will be the only moment of the day that the temperature is comfortable and we should take advantage of it. Beck steps up beside me on the tracks and looks back the way we came with a frown on his face so I nudge him with my elbow.

"You're not really worried Boyd's still coming after us, are you?"

He shoots me a quick look but turns back to scan the distance while answering me.

"I honestly don't know. He's got no transportation as far as I know and it'd be suicide for him to come out here on foot. All I can say is the more miles we put between us and him, the better I'll feel."

I take my own look back and nod my head. Even if Boyd's no longer a threat, the faster we go the less water we'll use and the quicker we will know if the valley is going to work for us. I stretch my arms above my head to try and limber the ache from them but then grin and give him a small shove.

"Rock, paper, scissors for who pumps first?"

I see the twinkle come into his eyes but he shakes his head.

"No way! I pump first."

I look at him with suspicion and slowly ask, drawing out the word, "Why?"

The twinkle in his eyes morphs into amusement and he starts backing towards the cart. "Cause then you'll have to pump in the heat, not me!"

I lunge towards the door with a laugh but he beats me to it and sticks out his tongue at me. It feels good to laugh for a change even though we know both of us will be pumping in the high heat at some point today. Beck disengages the brakes from the control panel and gets us moving while Glo and I pull out food for our meager breakfast. We use up the last of the pre-filled wraps saving one for Beck and grumble while eating them. The tortillas have gone soggy and the vegetables inside them are basically mush but they fill us up even if they don't taste that great. I promise Glo we can have some jam roll ups as a treat for lunch and pack the rest of the food away. We can have the same meal we had for supper as we had yesterday but after that, I'll have to find something to make from the ration boxes.

We only used half the engine charge before calling it a night so Beck only has to pump for an hour to top it off and switch back over to the engine. We spend the next few hours while the engine speeds us along studying the rail maps. Our fingers follow the broken lines on the map to faraway cities and towns that we might be able to reach if the valley is dry. We calculate distances and travel times to get to other places but we both know it won't really matter. Neither of us knows anything about the conditions out there but if the government stopped the ration and water stations in our state then there's a good chance it stopped in all the other southern states too. The only two option we really have is the valley or the north and with the labor camps the only way to get food and water now, we both agree north isn't an option.

The day's heat settles over us again just as the engine starts to slow. I give Beck a fake growl as I take my place behind the handle and start pumping. He sends me back a cheeky wink. The only good thing I can say about it is that my muscles warm up and don't ache quite so much with the exercise. This day seems to drag on and on. With nothing to see outside that changes the landscape, every minute feels like an hour. We pump and then sit in silence while the engine runs and then pump again. The small lunch of jam roll ups and a handful of peanuts and dried fruit only breaks up the day by a few minutes. The most excitement we have is when Glo spots the second junction and we pass by it. There's nothing interesting about it. No buildings of any kind, just the tracks splitting off in a different direction.

Beck's at the handle pumping late in the afternoon and I'm trying to nap on the bench to pass the time when Glo lets out a yell.

"Hey, guys? There's something ahead!"

Right away I feel the speed decrease as Beck cranes his head to get a look ahead. I look to the charging meter as I roll off the bench and see it's in the green with two bars to go until it's full. If whatever is ahead is a danger to us then at least we can have a bit of speed to try and get through it fast. I join Glo at the front windows and strain my eyes to see what's out there. I can just make out some sort of large structure over the tracks but I don't think it's a building, more like an arch of some kind. What concerns me is what's on the ground by the tracks. I cup my hands around my eyes to try and see further but we just aren't close enough for me to make out what it is.

I pat the messenger bag that I always wear now and feel the heavy outline of my grandfather's revolver. It comforts me and fills me with dread all at the same time. Firing it the first time at Boyd was pure instinct. I'm not sure I could deliberately take someone's life if I had time to think about it first. Glo slides her small hand into mine and gives it a squeeze. I look down at her head and realize that I could and I would pull the trigger if it means she will be safe.

We're close enough now that I can make out the shapes of tents scattered on either side of the tracks but it's the thin trails of smoke rising into the air that fills me with dread. The only reason for smoke like that is cooking fires and that means people. The thought is immediately confirmed when I see figures racing towards the tracks from either side. I keep my eyes glued to them as I yell out.

"Beck! Brake, Beck! Braaaaake!"

He yells back, "I'm trying!"

Glo and I are thrown forward against the glass when the brake engages. I catch myself from bashing my face against it in time but Glo doesn't and she bounces off and flies backward with a grunt. I want to drop down and check on her but I can't tear my eyes away from what's ahead of us. We're getting closer with every second and I can now make out the faces of the men that are filling the track ahead and they look angry. I can see their mouths moving in shouts but I can't hear them. The message they're shouting is clear enough though. They want us to stop and the many guns and arrows pointing towards our cart tell me that grandfather's revolver is not going to make any difference in this fight.

I drop down to the floor of the cart, defeated, and pull Glo into my lap while I wait for the impact. She's dazed from the blow to her face and blood is pouring out of her nose. I try and stem the flow with my sleeve as I look up to Beck. He's got his feet planted hard and he's leaning back with his hands clenched white around the handle like he can stop the cart with just his will to do so. I've never seen the expression on his face before. His lips are peeled back, with his teeth showing, making him look fierce like he's ready to fight.

I close my eyes expecting to feel an impact through the paneling at my back but it doesn't come when the cart comes to a stop. I can hear them yelling now through the open windows for us to come out and my eyes fly open when someone bangs against the cart. I see Beck take a stomping step towards the door and scramble to my feet pulling Glo up with me.

"NO! Beck, wait!"

He turns his head towards me and I suck in a breath at how empty his eyes are. I finally realize just how much this brief freedom meant to him now that he's about to lose it again. I rush toward him while pulling Glo with me and push her into his arms and then drag the strap of the messenger bag over my head and drop it at his feet.

"Wait, Beck. Just wait. Listen to me!" When I see he's back and focused on me, I go on. "I need you to stay on the cart. You have to keep Glo safe. Do you understand? I'll try and talk to them but if it goes wrong and they won't listen or they grab me, then I need you to turn the engine back on and just try and get through. Stay down on the floor if they start shooting but don't stop no matter what. The most important thing is that you keep Glo safe!"

He starts shaking his head and opens his mouth to argue but I'm already moving around him towards the door and he's got Glo slumped in his arms so he can't reach for me. I shove the door open and take a quick glance back at the girl who owns my heart before yelling.

"I'm coming out! Don't shoot!"

I take a hesitant step down and feel my legs turn to jelly as I take in all the rifles and arrows pointed my way. I swallow hard and step the rest of the way down, closing the door behind me. There are too many of them yelling at both me and at the others to come out of the cart. I can't single out who's in charge, so I just take a deep breath and channel the strongest woman I've ever known, Abuela.

"HEY! Stop yelling at me or at least do it one at a time!" I yell back at them.

It must surprise or shock them that I'm not cowering on the ground because they all become silent and I know it's not because I intimidate them in any way. I scan their faces and zero in on the only one who doesn't look angry. He's got a slight smirk on his face and amusement in his eyes so I talk just to him, ignoring the rest.

"We don't want any trouble. We're just passing through!"

His eyebrows shoot up like I've somehow surprised him and he shrugs one shoulder.

"Well, that's good to know Chica, but this is our land that you're passing through so that is a problem. Tell the other two to come out here and maybe we can talk about passage."

His tone of voice tells me this is a joke to him but I'm not finding any of it funny.

"No. They're staying inside so tell me what you want so we can be on our way."

I take a step back when he lets out a bark of laughter. I watch him closely but his rifle is pointing at the dirt by my feet and not at my heart so I hope that means he's not about to shoot me. A few of the other men laugh as well but their weapons stay firmly pointed in my direction.

"I admire your bravery. Here you are, outnumbered, and you think you can dictate terms to us?"

I don't know what to say to that. It's not bravery, it's a desperate bluff but before I can say anything else, the man I was speaking to is pushed aside and a very old man shuffles past him and comes right up to me. He studies my face for a moment, hums at the back of his throat and then nods.

"It's called, moxie! She comes by it naturally."

I'm frozen in uncertainty at his words and the grin that spreads across his face but it's his next words that give me hope that we will get out of this mess.

"You have Bonita's eyes. Are you her granddaughter, child?"

Chapter Eighteen

I'm stunned for words at his question so I just nod my head. He pats me on the shoulder and steps past me to lay a hand on the cart and lets out a cackle of laughter.

"I'd recognize old Tilly here anywhere! I swear Lucas spent more time in this thing than he did in his own home." He turns back to me with a face creased with happiness. His eyes look past me to the men still pointing their weapons at me and he barks at them, "Enough of that! This is the granddaughter of old friends of mine. You will treat her with the same respect you would show an honored guest!"

I watch in disbelief as most of the men seem to melt away but don't miss the angry and suspicious looks some of them directed my way as they go. The original man I had spoken to walks towards me with his amused expression and holds out his hand.

"Sorry about that, strangers aren't very welcome around here. I'm John Welshe and that's my father, Charlie. He seems to think he knows you or knows your people?"

I reach out and shake his hand while shaking my head. "Claudia. He knows my grandparent's names so..."

He frowns down at our joined hands and tugs me closer.

"Is that blood? Are you hurt?"

I yank my hand from his and spin around to the door to go check on Glo and Beck but stop in my tracks as I see Charlie helping my small sister down the steps. Beck is hovering behind her while nervously looking all around. When his eyes land on mine, I give him a cautious nod that it's ok to come down. Glo barrels into me and wraps her skinny arms around my waist. Her voice is muffled against my chest when she speaks.

"My ose urts!"

I blow out a breath of relief and gently push her away from me to inspect her face. She looks ghastly with dried blood running in tracks down either side of her mouth and her tiny nose is swollen but it looks like the bleeding has stopped for now. I flinch when a hand comes my way but it's just John holding out a wet handkerchief. He motions it towards Glo's face so I take it with a small smile of thanks and wipe away as much of the sticky blood as I can. Charlie steps up beside us and peers down at her before his eyes go wide in surprise.

"OH! You're just a little girl! With all that war paint on your face, I thought you were a fierce warrior come to do battle with my tribe," he teases. Glo's giggle does more to settle my nerves than his teasing words. He turns to me and waves at the cart. "Why don't you have your friend move Tilly down to the bridge? I would be honored if you all joined me and my family for an early supper and you can catch me up on the news of your family."

I look past him at Beck who nods in agreement. We would both feel more secure if we can move the cart to the other side of all these people. So I take the arm Charlie's offered me and with Glo clutching my other hand, we walk towards his camp as he tells me the history of his relationship with my grandparents.

"Lucas was a good friend of mine for many years. We met before he and Bonita got married. I thought he was a sun-touched white man when he told me he was prospecting for gold in the Black Mountains. That gold rush ended back in the nineteen forties but he was determined to find his lucky strike and sure enough, that crazy paleface found it! For years he would stop at the Avi on his way in and out of the mountains, so we were close friends. I was the manager and ran things back then so I always had the same suite ready for him. After he married Bonita, she would come with him sometimes. I haven't seen her since Lucas's funeral, though."

He chuckles when I ask him, "What's an Avi?"

"Oh, well that was the tribe's Casino resort!" He laughs at my confused expression and explains. "A casino was a place where people would go to gamble their money. It had a resort hotel with fancy pools and a golf course. People would vacation there. Now, it's where most of us live. Once the river was mostly dried up and the wars began, the tourists dried up too. No one had any money for vacations or gambling so our people moved into the resort to be close to what's left of the river. The government is gone from here so we do what we want now and grow enough crops on what used to be the golf course to sustain us."

I look around the area but all I see is desert and scrub in all directions except for ahead where a bridge is.

"Where is this place? Why are you all out here?"

He takes the time to wave and nod at some of the people we are passing but they all continue to look at Glo and me with suspicion.

"Avi is twelve miles south of us." We're on the way back from Laughlin. There's a trading post there once a month. We go to share news, trade supplies and barter for rations sometimes.

I look at him in surprise. "The government is still giving out rations here?" I ask with hope. Maybe we can find a place nearby instead of going all the way to the valley.

He snorts a laugh. "No, there hasn't been a station around here for years. The closest ration station was in Vegas but the news we got yesterday was that they've closed all of them now. Too bad, there used to be a guy with a truck that would bring people down from there to trade."

I let out a disappointed breath. "Yeah, they shut ours down too. That's why we had to get away. The gangs in our town were going on a rampage stealing everyone's water and rations."

He makes that humming noise in the back of his throat before speaking. "It's the way of the world now. The strong take from the weak. Tell me, why are you out here alone? Where is your mother or grandmother?"

I bite my lip as an image of Abuela laying in a pool of blood fills my mind. I try to swallow the anguish down but it sticks in my throat. It's Glo who answers him.

"Abuela died two days ago. The gangs got her but she saved us so we could escape!"

He looks sharply at me to confirm her words so I just nod with tears in my eyes. "She did, she prepared us to leave but the gang attacked before we could get away and they…they shot her. Our home is gone now, burned to the ground."

He stops and turns me to face him putting one of his hands on my shoulder and one on Glo's.

"I'm so sorry for your loss. Bonita was a wonderful woman. You were both blessed to have her in your lives. Where is her daughter, your mother?"

I shrug my shoulders. "She left us with Abuela when I was eight and Glo was just one. She went north to find my grandfather's people. It's just been the three of us ever since."

He shakes his head in sadness. "You are orphans now with no family but each other. Where are you going?"

I look away from him and try to think of a way to ask if we could stay somewhere around here but Glo pipes up and lets all our secrets out.

"We're going to see a waterfall with a pool I can swim in! I've never been in water before! Do you think there will be fish? I hope there are fish. I've never seen fish either."

I let out a groan as she tells this total stranger our biggest secret but he just throws back his head and laughs. He sees my distress and holds up a hand.

"No, no, don't worry child! I know of the place she speaks of. Like I said, Lucas and I were good friends. I arranged delivery of many of the materials Lucas needed to build his home there as well as the rental of the hover sleds he used to get it all into the valley."

My mouth drops open in shock. "You've been there? You've seen it? It really exists?" I had bet on it being there but a small part of me never really believed until this moment. Just as fast as hope flares in me his frown and words take it away.

"Well, no actually. I haven't been there myself. I wasn't all that interested in hiking through the mountains but he told me all about it and like I said, I helped coordinate all the supplies he hauled in for the house. I know he was heartbroken when Bonita refused to relocate there. I can't say I blamed her, though. It's very isolated. It's a good choice for you now. That isolation is a good thing with all the troubles in the world."

I shake my head in disagreement. "What if we travel all the way there and the water is gone like everywhere else? Is that a chance I can afford to take with her life? What about here? Is there a place we could settle here? With your people?"

His shoulders slump and with sadness in his eyes, he reaches up and cups my cheek.

"I'm sorry, that isn't an option. If it was up to me alone I would take you in for the sake of my friendship with your grandparents but it's not up to me. The band voted to not let any outsiders in. There was just too much bad trouble at the start of the wars. There's a lot of anger in my people. They wouldn't allow it. I'm sorry."

I nod my head in understanding and turn away. We are on our own.

Chapter Nineteen

Boyd has no choice but to swallow down the acid of anger that keeps creeping up his throat. They've traveled over two hundred miles and still haven't caught up with his brother and the girl. Marco and Pete have lost faith in him and he can hear the disrespect in their tones every time they speak to him now. What should have been a triumphant day turned into one headache after another. Already miserable from an uncomfortable night spent out in the desert with only a tarp to protect them from the bugs and constantly blowing sand, they were then forced to sit around waiting for the buggy to charge up. They had finally started up again when not two hours into the journey, a tire blew out. It was then that Marco started making noise about returning to town with Pete agreeing with him.

Boyd shut them down even though he was ready to quit too. The problem they didn't see was, what then? They could return to town and live off of what they'd looted from the other residents but what would they do once it all ran out? With the ration stations closing, there would be nothing coming into the town and most of the people would either leave or die. He needed to look to the future and the only future he could see was going north and finding a way over that wall. The only way over the wall was money which led him right back to the girl.

He looks around at the passing landscape of...nothing. There's nothing out here for her to run to. She has to be going to one of her grandfather's claims for gold. She, like everyone else, has no hope of making it down here in the south so she must have a plan to get the funds to go north. There could be no other reason for her to take a kid out in this desert that he could think of. It had to be to get gold and he hadn't come this far to give up on it now.

Pete interrupts his thoughts from the back seat. "Boss, we only have enough water for a few more days. If we don't find them by tonight, we'll have no choice but to turn back."

A growl of frustration escapes Boyd and he barks back, "Then we cut back on how much we drink. We are NOT going back until we find that girl!"

Marco takes his eyes off the way ahead and sends him a look of disbelief. "You can't be serious! Listen, I know you want revenge for what she and your brother did but it's not worth dying over!"

The contempt in his voice has Boyd's anger reaching a boiling point. "Stop the buggy!" When Marco ignores him and keeps driving, Boyd pulls the gun from his waistband and holds it to his head.

"STOP...THE...BUGGY!"

Marco slams on the brakes causing all of them to lurch forward. Once they come to a stop, Boyd orders them out.

"Let's talk about dying out here or back in the town because if we don't find that girl, that's what we're facing!" He shook his head and spit at their feet at the dumb looks on their faces.

"What do you think's going to happen once we run out of rations back home? The stations are closed for good so what we got back there is it. Once it's gone, there's not going to be anyone around to take more from. We have no choice but to go north and I don't know about you two but I'm not going to be anyone's slave! I'm getting over that damn wall to the good life no matter what it takes." He takes a heaving breath and waves his gun to the east. "She came out here for a reason and the only reason I can come up with is to go to her grandfather's claims for the gold he used to mine. We NEED that GOLD! So I'm going to keep after her until I catch up, even if it takes every damn drop of water we have to do it!" He waves the gun back to point at them.

"You two are either with me or you can walk back. You decide right here, right now!"

Pete and Marco share a look but both nod in agreement. Marco holds up a hand.

"We're with you, Boss! Neither one of us wants to go to the labor camps. You're right, the gold is the key. We just forgot about it, that's all!"

Boyd lets out a long-suffering sigh at being saddled with these two idiots but nods his head and waves them back into the buggy, catching the looks of concerned relief that the two share. He trudges back around the front end to the passenger door when Pete calls out.

"Hey! What's that?"

Boyd looks up at where Pete's standing in the back seat, staring off into the distance with a hand shading his eyes. He climbs into the buggy and stands on the seat to get a look at what his man has spotted and starts to grin. For the first time on this journey, the landscape has changed. He can't make out exactly what it is but it looks like there's movement out there. Even if it's not the girl and his brother, it might be someone who saw them. He grins at his men.

"Let's go. It's hunting time!"

Chapter Twenty

❝How are you set for water?" Charlie asks us when Beck has joined us again.

I think about how much I should tell this guy but then I just give up worrying about it. He seems to know everything anyway.

"We've gone through some of it but I hope we will have enough to get back to the cart if the valley is dry."

He nods. "We will exchange your empty jugs for full ones to help with that."

I look over towards the river. "Thank you for the offer but can't we fill them up from the river?"

He shakes his head in caution. "No, it must be boiled and strained to make it safe to drink. We have plenty of treated water to gift you a few jugs and we'll be home in the morning where we have a large treatment station set up."

Before I can thank him for the generous gift, his son John walks up with a concerned frown.

"Sorry to interrupt, Dad but we're going to have to move on today after all. There's a windstorm heading this way."

I look at him in surprise and awe then look all around at the quiet, still desert that surrounds us.

"How do you know that? Are there some kind of signs on the land that tell you that?"

He gives me a strange look before pulling a thin, black, shiny box from his pocket and holds it up for me to see.

"Uh, no. Satellite weather app?"

He says it like I should know what that means so I just nod like I get it. Charlie sees right through me and laughs.

"Old tech, child! We still have a few toys that help us out. Many of our older people had university educations and know how to hack past the North's firewalls to get us information we can use." My face must still show confusion at words I've never even heard before because he tries again.

"They went to schools before the wars and know how to use the tech. The north still has everything we used to have so we use their satellites to help us down here in the south."

Ok, that I understand, so I ask John a question maybe he can answer. "Can your box tell you where the government is still handing out rations? Maybe we could go there?"

John looks at his Dad with a sad expression before answering. "I'm sorry Claudia, they've closed all the stations. The only choice people have now is to go to the labor camps for rations or try and find a way to survive out here. To be honest, I'm surprised they lasted as many years as they did. You could try northern Utah. I've heard that there are still some communities farming there but it's a very religious area with strict rules. I'm sorry I can't help you more than that."

Charlie pats his son on the back and sends him to get us some water jugs while I think about everything he's said. The only choices we have are the same as when we left home, the valley or north to the camps. I have a flash of an image of my mother laying on cool, green grass on the other side of the wall and feel burning anger at her for abandoning us. I shake the image away and focus back on Glo and Beck. There has to be another option.

"How do you get over the wall?"

His expression turns to pity as he shakes his head. "Many, many people have been asking that question for years now. There's only two ways that I know of. They'll take you if you have a high degree of education but you'll spend the rest of your life working for them to pay your passage over. The other way is if you have enough money to bribe one of the wall guards to smuggle you through but it would take huge amounts and our dollar is worthless." He looks down at Glo and then at Beck and I. "Go to the valley. If it's dry…head north and try and find a community to take you all in. That's your only choice now if you won't go to the camps."

He looks around at the activity in his camp that has picked up in the last few minutes as people started pulling down tents and packing up their belongings.

"We had planned to stay here tonight and travel the rest of the distance to Avi tomorrow but with the storm on the way, we will be leaving shortly. I'm afraid we will no longer be able to have a meal together. I'm sorry, I was looking forward to hearing more of your grandmother but perhaps it's best if you get going. Coyote Rock is less than a hundred miles from here. That's where Lucas always left Tilly and went into the mountains on foot. I went and brought the cart back to your grandmother after Lucas was found. You know to take the next junction where the tracks split? If you don't switch, they curve south and go deeper into Arizona on the way to Mexico. I can tell you there's nothing left alive that way."

Beck steps forward with his hand out. "Thank you, sir, for the water and the information. We'll let you get packing and be on our way."

I echo his words and offer my own hand to shake but Charlie pulls both me and Glo into a fatherly hug. When we pull back, he has tears in his kind eyes.

"I'm so sorry I can't…"

His words are interrupted by men yelling out in concern, causing all of us to turn and look in the direction of the commotion. I feel a cold shiver race down my spine when I realize they're pointing at the direction we came from. I feel Beck put a hand on my shoulder from behind and turn to see him start stepping back with fear in his eyes. He reaches out and snags Glo's arm and pulls her with him as he moves back further towards where our cart is waiting. I'm shaking my head in confusion at him when he says one word that has me moving too.

"Boyd!"

Charlie grabs my arm as I try and move past him. "What? What is Boyd?"

I see Beck scoop up Glo and run for the cart so I turn back and watch as Charlie's men form a line between their camp and some kind of vehicle that's heading towards us alongside the tracks. I'm only half relieved by all the rifles and bow and arrows that are starting to be aimed at whoever is traveling this way. A shake of my arm has me meeting Charlie's eyes and I swallow hard before answering.

"Boyd is the leader of the gang that attacked us and killed Abuela. Beck is his younger brother and he betrayed Boyd to get us to safety. If it's him, he's coming for his revenge!"

Charlie gives me a hard nod and the grip he has on my arm turns into a push.

"Go, go now. Whoever it is, my men will hold them off until you are away. Good luck, Claudia!"

I stand frozen for a heartbeat as he strides away barking out orders but then I hear Glo yelling my name so I turn and sprint toward the cart. We need to get out of here and put as much distance between us and whoever that is. I can't really believe that Boyd would travel so far after us just to get revenge but I'm not willing to stick around and find out.

I fly up the steps and see Beck already standing by the control panel waiting for me to get on the cart. As soon as the door latches behind me, he hits the button to engage the engine and the cart starts moving with a lurch. I rush to the front windows while Beck goes to the back ones. I see the bridge a few feet ahead and it spans a deep river basin that has only a small stream of dirty water running through the center of it where once a mighty river flowed that provided life to millions of people. The wooden ties that support the steel tracks are white with age and I wish I had thought to ask Charlie if the bridge was still strong enough to support the weight of the cart and us in it. I look down at Glo who's come up beside me and pull her against me. If we crash through this thing then I hope it's over quick for all of us. Our speed increases, sending us out over the basin as I hold my breath and squeeze my eyes shut. I swear I can hear the beams under us creaking and groaning with every revolution of the wheels. Glo laughs and claps her hands making me open my eyes and releasing the stale air in my lungs. We've made it over the bridge and are back on solid ground.

I squeeze her against me for a second and then turn and rush back to the other end to see if we're being followed by whoever was approaching the camp. Beck's got both of his palms pressed against the glass and his lips are a hard, thin line as the group we just left gets smaller and smaller the further we travel.

"What did you see?" I ask him.

He shakes his head and blows out a breath, never taking his eyes off of the scene in the distance.

"I think it is Boyd. Look! They're backing up. I think they're leaving!"

I push closer to the glass, trying to make out what's happening and see the vehicle moving further away from Charlie's people. I'm about to smile in relief when the car or whatever it is makes a wide arc around the men standing between us and them and then heads back towards the river.

"They can't get across without the bridge, right?" I plead desperately as we watch it turn again and travel parallel to the river until they disappear from sight.

Beck pushes off the window and turns to slump back against it.

"I don't know. I don't know if there's another way across it. I can't believe he followed us! What does he want? Why can't he just let me go? It's not like he ever cared about me. I was just his dog to kick when he felt like it."

I bite my lip in uncertainty. What could the guy want if not his brother? I wrack my brain to try and figure out what would drive Boyd to travel so far for but come up empty.

"Are you sure it was your brother?"

His jaw tightens and he crosses his arms in anger. "Yeah, he stood up when they came to a stop to talk to those men. I'd recognize him anywhere."

My own anger surges. "What does he want from us? Did you take something from him?"

Beck goes to snap at me but pulls it back and just shakes his head tiredly instead. He looks down the cart at Glo before facing me.

"No, I didn't take anything from him except you. He wanted you and he wanted the supplies he thinks you have. You should just let me off here. Maybe I can stop him and convince him to turn back. I'll tell him you don't have hardly any supplies."

I reach out and punch him in the arm. "I'm not doing that! Like Glo said, we're a family now and family sticks together. If he finds a way across the river and manages to catch up to us, we'll deal with him together."

He rubs the spot on his arm that my boney knuckles connected with and gives me a small smile.

"Together?"

I roll my eyes and nod. "Yes, you idiot, together! Now, let's go see where we're headed."

I walk back to the front with Beck following and we line up at the windows. The landscape has changed since we crossed over the river. There are quite a few abandoned buildings in the distance on either side of us and the land ahead is rising. The biggest change though is the mountains I can see straight ahead of us, growing taller with every mile we travel toward them. That's our destination. Somewhere, deep in those mountains is the secret valley and hopefully our new home. We just have to make it there.

Glo and I stay at the front windows as we climb up the gentle hills toward the mountains that are getting closer. Neither of us has ever seen anything but flat land and we are fascinated by the changes even though it still just sand, scrub, and rock. Just slightly bigger rocks on an incline. Beck returned to the back windows to watch for his brother in case he found a way across the river. There's still a little more than an hour left on the engine charge and then we'll have to start pumping again. I know we'll have a harder time on these hills. Most likely, both Beck and I will have to pump together to make any real speed but the sun will be down in a few more hours so we'll do what we have to, to make as much distance from the river as possible.

"Día, what's that?" I follow the direction Glo is pointing and my eyes flare wide. "Beck! Beck, get back here!"

I hear his boots pound our way so I just point.

"Oh, God!"

His exclamation says it all. The black mass heading our way is an act of God. It's the sandstorm John said was coming and at the rate we're going it'll be less than an hour before we collide with it. I turn to face Beck but before I can ask him what we should do, a gust of wind from the open windows blows half my hair into my face and I hear the sound of blowing sand and small rocks scratch against the outside of the cart.

"We need to close the windows and hope there's some cover ahead!"

Beck nods with fear in his eyes and rushes away. Before I go to help him, I turn and look at the force of nature we are headed for one more time and then past it to the mountains. We were so close!

Chapter Twenty-One

Boyd points ahead through the spiderwebbed windshield, ignoring the moaning from the back seat.

"There! It looks like it was a boat launch or something. Go there, we'll find a way up on the other side once we cross the stream."

Marco's lips are pulled back with his teeth showing against the pain in his shoulder where an arrow bobs with every jolt the buggy makes. All he wants to do is stop, get out and pull the arrow from his throbbing wound and then try and save Pete's life. His friend is bleeding out in the back seat from the bullet he took to the chest when those men had opened up on them. He silently curses Boyd for the fool that he is. Who mouths off to a larger group of men with that many weapons pointed at them? If it was up to him, he would have turned around right then and there and forgotten all about the girl and the gold. The sharp jab of Boyd's gun in his side reminds him that he isn't in charge and that he now no longer has any choices.

"I said turn there!" Boyd snarls at him before removing the barrel from his side and jabbing it towards the direction he wants Marco to drive to. "We can't let them get too far this time. We almost have them!"

Marco doesn't reply but turns in the direction the man wants. He will follow along for now but when his chance comes, he will take that gun from Boyd and leave his corpse for the coyotes. He doesn't care about the girl or the gold anymore. He just wants to go back to town and when the food runs out, they could make a plan from there. He's not going to die alone all the way out here on a fool's errand.

The buggy navigates down the old river bank and the small stream with ease but the rougher terrain has him screeching in agony as the arrow stuck in him waves back and forth. He wants to reach up and pull it out but he's afraid the blood loss will do him in and then Boyd will shove him out and keep going. He has no choice but to leave it in until they're forced to stop. The charge will only last another hour or so and then he can patch himself up and take on Boyd. From the lack of moaning from Pete, he assumes his friend is gone and he'll be on his own.

It takes a while to find a way out of the river basin and then get back to the train tracks. They've been traveling for almost an hour since they lost sight of the weird train car they are chasing. The terrain has changed to uphill as they head east through abandoned buildings and Marco watches as the charge meter starts to drop faster as the small buggy is forced to work harder. He leans forward off of his seat to try and get some air to cool his sweat soaked back and feels a wave of dizziness wash over him. He doesn't realize that the arrow in his shoulder has gone all the way through and all the bobbing of the shaft has widened the exit wound causing his lifeblood to pour out down his back at a faster rate.

Black wings fill his vision at the edges of his eyes and he jolts when Boyd reaches out and yanks the steering wheel back on course from where it has started to drift. His head clears long enough to understand the words being shouted at him.

"Pull over to that building!"

He turns his head slowly in the direction Boyd is pointing and sees a cinderblock building with no windows, just a door, so turns the wheels to drive towards it. Relief fills him at the thought of stopping and tending to his wound. The pain in his shoulder has muted to numbness and his arm and hand are incredibly weak. He needs to remove the arrow before he has a permanent injury to the nerves and muscles in his arm. His head is cloudy so he only caught half of what Boyd is saying but enough of it to follow his directions.

"Stop here! I'm going to lay out the tarp. You need to drive over the edge of it as close to the building as possible so it's anchored by the wheels. We'll wrap it over the buggy and tie it off on the other side."

Marco just nods his head, not really understanding why they are doing that but knowing they will be stopped soon so he does as instructed. Boyd waves him forward when he has the tarp where he wants it. As soon as he calls out to stop, Marco shuts the machine down and just leans back against the seat with his head resting on the headrest and closes his eyes. He hears Boyd yelling and cursing at him but he feels like he's floating and it's so soothing that he just ignores him. Minutes later, he is yanked from the pleasantness by a roaring pain when Boyd grabs him and drags him across the seats and out the passenger door. The pain is so intense that all he can do is lay there in the dirt and listen to Boyd bang around while the wind rustles with the tarp. The wind is nice and cools his hot, wet back as he lays there waiting for the pain to subside. It had just started to fade back to numbness when he feels Boyd start pulling his arms again and dragging him along the ground.

Marco bellows out a soul shaking scream as the arrow catches on a rock and it tears a wider gash in his body. This time, it's a white light that flares behind his eyes and his last thought is, no amount of gold is worth this.

Chapter Twenty-Two

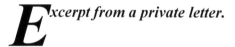

Excerpt from a private letter.

May 3, 2029

My dearest Bonita,

It's been over two months since I've seen your beautiful eyes and I miss them so much. All of this, the distance between us and the hard work has paid off, making it worthwhile. I struck the biggest vein to date at the second claim and have pulled more gold out of it than the entire first claim. We will never have to work again and our children will be able to live in luxury.

I have put so much time into this vein that the work on our house in the valley took longer to complete than I thought it would but I'm happy to say that it is now finished! On my next trip out, I will focus on bringing all the furnishing and household goods to fill it so that it will be ready for your arrival.

I know you are resistant to the idea of bringing the baby here to live but it may be our only option if we lose the war. I'm hearing rumors of a wall that is being constructed to cut us off from the north. If we lose and they build it, life will become incredibly hard for everyone in the south and it won't matter how much gold we have. Water is already getting scarce for the farmers so without food shipments from the north, people will begin to starve. I fear for our lives if we don't make plans.

I've spoken to Charlie about it and he's in agreement that things look bleak for us southerners. When I passed through, Avi was like a ghost town. The slot machines and tables were empty and they've been forced to drain and close all but the smallest pool. He told me that the council has plans if we lose the war to close the resort to the public and move the band members into it so they can be closer to the river. He even said there was talk of ripping up the golf course to plant crops! Can you imagine that? A PGA rated course turned into farmland!

I'm confident that if the worst should happen, we would be able to be self-sufficient and comfortable in the valley. I understand all the reasons you don't want to come but we may not have a choice so I would be willing to discuss bringing another family with us if we are forced to flee.

Please consider it, sweetheart. I couldn't bear to see you and our child suffering from the lack of resources if we lose the war.

I plan to head out and back to you both next week and look forward to being a family once again.

Your loving husband,

Lucas

"There! Start braking, Beck!" I yell over my shoulder to be heard over the roar of the wind and the constant pings of rocks and sand that are blasting the cart. I can just barely make out a dip in the tracks that are bracketed by tall rocks on either side ahead of us. We need to get behind some kind of cover or the wind will tip us over.

As if my thoughts are prophetic, we are hit by a gust so strong that I feel the left side of the cart start to tilt up.

"Move to the left side!" Beck screams, but I'm already moving. I grab Glo where she is huddling on the floor in front of the forward-facing windows with her hands covering her ears and her eyes squeezed tightly shut and drag her with me to the left side shelves and cling to them. I'm whispering frantic prayers that our combined weight will be enough to bring the wheels on this side back down onto the track. What feels like minutes later but is only a few seconds, we all feel the steel wheels clunk back down and the screeching of the brakes ring out. Glo and I are thrown forward against the front windows of the cart and I groan in frustration when I see we have stopped at the top of the dip that will hopefully protect us from the storm's crazy winds.

I shove away from the windows and lunge back towards the handle. "Pump! We stopped too soon!"

Beck and my hands hit the handle at the exact same time with a hard push but it's locked tight and won't budge. I let out a very nasty curse word that has Beck's eyes flaring wide in shock but they clear quickly when he realizes the problem.

"The brake's still on! Hold on."

He reaches down and struggles with the lever but finally gets it to move and release the brake. As soon as I see it flip over I start pumping the handle. There is so much resistance that I think that the brake hasn't released all the way but then understand that I'm fighting against the wind to make the cart move. Beck adds his muscle to it and we finally manage to go the fifteen feet we need to move to be down in the dip with the rocks on both sides. The noise level of the wind drops by at least half and the near constant hail of rocks and sand hitting us goes from constant to occasional. I slump to the floor in relief and rest my forehead on the stationary handle as Beck sets the brakes again.

As my ears adjust to the new volume of noise, I can just make out the sound of Glo sobbing. I don't bother getting to my feet and just crawl the few feet to her and pull her off the floor and into my arms. She sobs against my shoulder while trying to talk.

"Wanna…go…home…no…more…adventure!"

I rub her back trying to soothe her but I have no words. I want to go home too. More than anything, I want to sob out my own tears at all that has happened in the past few days but I have to be strong for Glo so I gulp them back and just rest my head on hers, wishing for the thousandth time that Abuela was here with us. We sit like that for at least a half an hour with my legs going numb from her weight on them until all that's left of her sobs are a few hiccups. She finally lifts her swollen tear streaked face and whispers,

"I have to pee."

I let out a small laugh and cup her face using my thumbs to brush her tears away.

"Me too. Come on, let's go take care of that."

I rise to my feet on half asleep legs and turn towards the door. Beck's in our way and he's doing this weird tip toe dance.

"What on earth are you doing?" I ask in confused disbelief.

He answers us in a strained high pitch voice. "I have to go toooooooo!"

The giggle that erupts from Glo at his antics makes me realize that he's making a fool of himself for her benefit so I shake my head and send him a grateful smile.

"Well, get the door open so we can go then!" I laugh.

He sends me a wink and reaches out to open the door but it only moves a few inches before the wind slams it closed. He steps closer to the door and puts his shoulder into it but still only manages to open it a foot before letting the wind slam it closed again. He steps away from it and sighs before turning to us.

"I don't think it's a good idea to go out there right now. Even with the rocks protecting us, the wind is too strong."

Glo makes a strangled noise and bounces up and down with the need to go. I look around the cart and think for a minute before rummaging through the bags and boxes we brought with us. I empty out a small plastic bin that has a few jars of Abuela's homemade seasoning and jams in it and grab the one blanket we have. I hold them up for Beck and Glo to see and then shrug at their groans. We don't have a lot of choices here. Glo makes Beck stand in the corner facing away and she makes me sing loudly as I hold the blanket up to screen her while she does her business and then she does the same for me. It's uncomfortable and embarrassing but it gets the job done. I open one of the windows on the opposite side of the door where the wind isn't as strong and dump the contents out of the bin. I just hope the storm passes before we have to go again.

There's not a lot to do now that we're stuck here until the storm passes, so I divvy up the last of the cold soup and potatoes for our supper. With only a few tortillas, jam and dried fruit left in the basket I try and think about what we can eat tomorrow but my mind comes up blank. I have no way to cook any of the supplies we brought with us unless we build a fire so it'll be raw vegetables and cold protein. I put that worry aside for now and bring up the next one with Beck.

"Do you think Boyd is still after us?"

He swallows the last of his potato and frowns.

"I don't know. If they found another way to cross the river then maybe. But even if they did manage to cross, they'd be caught in this storm too. I don't know what that thing was that they were driving but it didn't look like it had a roof so they'd be completely exposed to the sand unless they found shelter somewhere." He shakes his head in annoyance. "He's stubborn but he's not suicidal so I think he might have turned back. At least, I hope he did."

I stare down into the last dredges of soup in my cup, thinking. I finally ask him what's really on my mind.

"If he didn't turn back and he catches up to us, are you going to be ok with me protecting us?"

His face fills with confusion. "What do you mean?"

I swallow hard but my voice is firm. "If he catches up to us, I'm going to kill him."

Beck's mouth drops open in shock but he snaps it closed and studies me for a moment.

"How do you plan on doing that?"

I place my hand on the messenger bag and decide it's time he knew what was inside of it.

"I have a gun. I shot Boyd the night he came to the house but it just wounded him. If he shows up, I won't wound him again, I'll kill him."

His eyes are huge as they track from my face to the bag and then back to my face. "You shot Boyd? You have a gun?"

I nod. "I won't let him hurt Glo. I'll do what I have to, to stop him. Can you live with that?"

He pushes to his feet and walks to the other end of the cart to stare out at the raging dust and sand that swirls around us. I look away and my eyes meet Glo's. She's chewing on her lip in uncertainty with tears in her eyes so I open my arms to her. She launches herself against me and clings tightly for a few moments before leaning back to look into my face.

"He's a really bad man, right? He killed Abuela?" At my sad nod, she takes a deep breath. "Then you wouldn't be a bad person if you shoot him again, right?"

Beck answers before I can. "No, she would be doing the right thing if she shot him again. If he catches up to us, the only thing we can do is stop him for good."

The look in his eyes breaks my heart. They are completely empty of any hope his brother would change into what a brother *should* be, so all I can do is nod with as much compassion in my own eyes as I can and hope I'm not forced to make good on my threat.

Chapter Twenty-Three

"Get up!" Boyd barks and uses his boot to kick at Marco's leg to get him moving but there's no response from the man.

He stands there in the dim light that's coming through a few cracks around the door of the concrete building they had taken shelter in the day before when the sand storm forced them to stop their hunt. He grunts in annoyance and turns away to open the door letting in more light. The storm passed in the night and the heat of the day is starting to build. Now that there's more light coming into the building, he can see the pool of drying blood Marco is laying in and that the man is no longer alive.

Rage fills him at all that the girl and his brother have cost him. His two most trusted men are dead and he's hundreds of miles from home. He stares down at Marco's body and considers turning back but shakes his head. Nothing's changed. There's still no future back there once the supplies run out. His only choice is to keep going and find the girl and make her give up the gold so he can go north for a better life. Revenge against her and his brother just sweetens the decision.

He turns his back on Marco's corpse and leaves the building without giving his dead man a second thought. Around the side of the building, the dune buggy waits. The tarp he had covered it with came halfway undone at some point during the storm, letting sand

and dust fill the driver's seat and foot well. Boyd mutters curses as he struggles with the last knot keeping the tarp secured. He finally loses his patience and just pulls out a knife and cuts the rope. When he throws the tarp back, a choked scream erupts from his mouth when he comes face to face with Pete's dead, staring eyes. He forgot that the man was still in the back seat. Flies and other insects crawled over the dead man's face as Boyd gets his breath back and racing heart under control.

The wound in his arm throbs as he struggles to pull the dead weight of Pete from the buggy and drag it into the building to lay beside Marco. His frustration and anger keep building as he clears the sand from the driver's area and finally boils over into a scream of rage when turning the key results in a warning buzzer. He almost pulls his gun and shoots the charge gauge when he sees that it only has a half red bar showing. Somehow, he manages to tamp down the violence roaring through his blood and instead pushes the buggy away from the wall of the building and out into the full sun to charge.

He knows it will take a few hours before it's ready to drive again so he settles down in the shade of the building and plots all the torture he's going to inflict on the two people responsible for his misery and then, he smiles.

Chapter Twenty-Four

When I open my eyes, the first thing I notice is the lack of sound. When we laid down last night to sleep, the wind was a constant roar that flung stones and sand at the cart. Now there is nothing but the sound of Glo's soft breathing and Beck's gentle snore. I sit up and try to ignore the ache in my body from pumping and sleeping on a hard, wooden floor for two days and nights. I wrinkle my nose from the smell in the cart. None of us have washed our bodies since leaving home and with all the windows closed the smell is ripe and pungent.

I move Glo's head off of my arm that she used as a pillow for the night and try and shake the pins and needles from it before getting to my feet. The windows on the left side and the front of the cart are all covered with a film of dust making it hard to see anything through them. The right side is cleaner so I look out and up and see blue sky above the rocks we had sheltered behind.

The storm is gone and I hope that means we will be able to make it to our stop today. With everything that happened yesterday afternoon, I hadn't kept track of how far we had gone once we crossed the river. For all I know, we could have missed the third junction. The idea of having to backtrack fills me with dread. I need to go outside and look around and do my morning business so I open the door and step down leaving it open to air the cart out a bit. Once

I'm done relieving myself, I walk around the cart and follow the tracks up the small hill and past the rocks where the land opens up again.

I stare at the mountains that don't seem very far away anymore. A smile creeps across my face. We must almost be there! I take a few more steps but the ground under my feet feels different so I look down with a frown. Instead of standing on the old wood and gravel between the steel tracks, my feet have sunk into a drift of sand. My eyes follow the ground ahead of me and instead of seeing the train tracks all I see is sand. My stomach drops when I realized we won't be able to go any further with the cart.

I just stand there staring down at the sand until I hear footsteps climbing the small hill behind me. Beck comes to a stop beside me and after a pause, curses.

"How far are the tracks covered?"

I shrug and hear him let out a sigh before he starts walking forward across the sand that covers the tracks. He keeps going for a hundred feet or so and then stops. Glo comes up beside me and slides her small arm through mine as we watch Beck start walking away from us again. She lets out a giggle and I look down at her to see what's funny but she's looking ahead so I ask,

"What's so funny?"

She points into the distance.

"Look, those rocks look like a howling dog!"

I see the rocks she's pointing at and make out the resemblance to a howling dog or wolf. It's neat how the landscape can form to look like different things but it doesn't help us...

"Coyote!"

Glo cocks her head to the side. "Yeah, I guess it could be a howling coyote."

Now it's my turn to laugh. "Coyote Rock! That's where Abuela said we get off the track and walk from. We almost made it!"

Beck makes his way back to us and I point out the distinctive rocks that are our destination.

"It won't be so bad to walk to. It doesn't look that far. It shouldn't take us more than a few hours to walk." I tell him.

He looks down at the cart and then back to the rocks in the distance and shakes his head.

"I think we should try and get the cart there. The tracks are only covered for about two hundred feet and then it looks clear. We should try and clear the sand."

I bark out a laugh. "Really? Sure, Beck. Let me just go get my broom and I'll have it swept away in a jiffy!"

He scowled at my sarcasm but just starts using his feet to try and shovel the sand away from the tracks. I throw up my hands.

"Beck! C'mon, there's no way we can move this much sand with just our feet. We don't have a broom or shovel to shift it, so unless the wind comes back…"

Something is tugging at my mind. Something Abuela had said to me about…air displacement! I don't know if it will work or not but it is worth a shot to save us the hours it would take to walk to Coyote Rock. We will be doing plenty of walking after we get there so why not try it? I turn away from him and head down the hill with Glo trailing behind me. I walk past the cart to the small trailer attached to the back of it and eye the hover sled. I walk all the way around it, releasing the clips that hold it in place and pop the remote out of the control panel where it's stored. I pull the sled off to the side of the trailer until it tips and slides to the ground, half leaning against the trailer. I brace it while Glo tugs on the bottom until I can lower it to the ground without it crashing.

Once it's on level ground, I fire it up with the remote and move it around the cart and back up the hill to where Beck is still dragging sand with his feet. He looks up, sees me coming with the sled and angrily crosses his arms.

"You're not even going to try and help me?" He snaps.

I ignore him and move the sled right at him until he's forced to move out of the way. Once I have it positioned over the area of track where I want it, I increase the lift power on the remote causing a cloud of sand and dust to billow out from under it. I let it run for a few minutes and then lower the power and move it ahead five feet. I look down at the cleared tracks and with a smug smile, toss the remote at Beck.

"Only one hundred and ninety-five feet to go. Enjoy!" I turn and head back down the hill with a giggling Glo.

"Hey! Where are you going?" He yells after me.

I don't look back just wave my hand in the air and call out,

"Breakfast!"

I laugh when I hear him groan but keep on going. I had seen a few things in the trailer when I'd pulled the sled off that would help me make some decent food. If we were going to be here for a while, I'm going to make a fire and cook enough food to last us the next few days while we are hiking.

Abuela had thought of everything. She had packed a box with kitchen pots and pans, a folding grate and two small canisters that have some kind of fuel in them with a thick wick in the center. It doesn't take me long to set up a little cooking area and with Glo's help, mix up some batter to make a batch of pan tortillas. I slice up some of the protein loaf and onions and cook it with some powdered eggs. I make enough to last the three of us for a few days and wrap it all up in the clothes and paper from the basket. It's bland food but it will give us the energy we will need to walk to the valley. I hope.

Once the food is ready, Glo and I eat quickly and then I send her back up the hill with a breakfast wrap for Beck and told her to tell him to stay up there while we clean up. Charlie's people had refilled our empty jugs of water so even though it was precious, I'm going to sacrifice a few inches of one jug to give Glo and I a quick wash. I just can't stand the smell or itchiness anymore. I wet one cloth and run the small bar of soap I had packed over it until I got a few bubbles. We share it so I doubt you could really call it getting clean, but at least I felt better. A second wet cloth wipes the soap off and I call it good. My scalp still itches but there is no way I can waste that much water to clean our hair. Once we are both dressed in clean clothes and all the cooking utensils are put away, I release the brakes and start pumping up the hill towards Beck. He's made a lot of progress while I cooked and cleaned. It looks like he has half the distance that needs to be cleared done. I set the brakes again and lay out a fresh cloth and the bar of soap for him so he can wash the smell off too. It's then that I realize that Beck doesn't have anything with him but the clothes on his back. He left home to warn us and he hadn't brought anything with him. He really has left everything behind.

I climb down from the cart and walk over to him with my hand held out.

"Here, I'll take over. I left you some soap and cloths to wash with. Um, if you give me your shirt and the soap when you're done, I'll wash it."

He looks at me in surprise before looking down at his shirt and then wincing. "Yeah, I guess it's pretty ripe. Do you think we should waste the water, though?"

I shake my head and take the remote from him. "I won't use much and it won't be really clean, but it will stink less and it will feel good to be cleaner, at least for a few hours."

He sends me a grateful smile but then turns and points to Glo with a stern finger. "I'm going to wash up. NO PEEKING!"

Her expression turns to outrage that he would think that she would, but then she sees his teasing eyes. She gives him a shove towards the cart and yells at him.

"Ewwww! Boys DO stink!"

I can't help but smile. As much as I had misgivings about Beck coming with us, he's doing wonders for Glo. His humor and teasing are helping her with the grief she is dealing with at the loss of Abuela. I'm really glad he is with us.

"C'mon, Glo. Let me show you how to work this thing so I can do stinky boy's laundry."

She makes a fake gagging sound but walks over to watch me. We clear ten feet of sand before I hand it over to her and I watch while she does another five before I'm satisfied she knows what she's doing. I walk back to the cart and call out so Beck knows I'm approaching. The last thing I want is to get an eyeful of naked Beck. Instead, I get an eyeful of a half-naked Beck! He opens the door and holds out his shirt, the wet soap and a jug of water but all I see is his bare chest. I feel my face flame up so I keep my eyes down and reach out to take the things he's holding out to me blindly. My eyes lift to his face once I have a grip on them and I see just how hard he's trying not to laugh at me so I snatch everything from him and spin away in embarrassment. Jerk!

I use one of the cooking pots from the trailer and add two inches of water to it until his shirt is barely wet enough to run the soap over it and then scrub it as best as I can with just my hands. Another two inches of water rinses it's as clean as I'm going to get it without using more water. I eye the jug and figure we've used just over half of it for breakfast and all of us cleaning up. I feel like it was worth it but I desperately hope that half of a jug of water won't mean the death of us at some point.

Sighing, I put the pot and soap away in the trailer and carry Beck's wet shirt over to where Glo is working. I spread his shirt out on the sled and figure it will be dry in ten minutes with the sun beaming down on it. I follow along with Glo as she clears the sand and moves forward to the next section but my mind drifts to the valley. It's so hard to make out any real details from the faded pictures so I fill in the blanks with my imagination. I picture the huge garden I will grow there. I'll make sure it's half in the shade of the valley walls so the sun won't burn it all dead. I'll be able to water it as much as I want and I can plant my citrus trees and see them grow tall and produce more fruit than ever.

We had only brought a few books with us so Beck and I will have to teach Glo about the world from what we can remember from school. I mindlessly turn his shirt over to dry on the other side as I keep thinking and realize that Glo and I will have to sacrifice a few of our clothes for Beck. I can rip the seams out and try and patch together another shirt and pair of shorts for him so he'd have at least one change of clothes. That gets me thinking of all the things we don't have and no way to get them. Maybe once we were settled Beck could go back to the river and see about trading at that market Charlie had mentioned. If I can grow enough food, we could use it to trade…

"All done! Now what?"

Glo's chirpy voice brings me out of my thoughts in surprise. The sand is cleared and all I can see into the distance is the steel track of the rails.

"Oh! Good job, Glo! I guess we go back to the cart and put the sled away. Then we can get going again."

She gives me a weird look and points behind me. I look over my shoulder and am even more surprised to see the cart right behind us. Beck must have brought it along as we cleared and I was so deep in thoughts of the valley that I didn't even hear it. Shaking my head at myself, I snatch his now dry shirt off of the sled and follow behind her to the trailer where I see him waiting for us. I toss the shirt at his bare chest. He catches it and lifts it up to his nose to take a sniff.

"Wow, much better! Thanks, Día. I really appreciate you washing this."

I mumble a "You're welcome" and wave towards the sled and trailer and for him to help me get it back up. He pulls the shirt over his head but not before I see the cheeky grin on his face at my uncomfortableness. Double Jerk!

Chapter Twenty-Five

We get moving and decide to use the engine for the last time to save our energy for the hike ahead of us. Thankfully, the tracks stay clear of any sand drifts and it's just under an hour later when Glo calls out that there's a junction ahead. The first two junctions we had passed kept us going straight ahead and this one's no different, which is a problem because we need to go in the other direction. We put on the brakes on as we pass where we need to get off and it takes a bit for Beck and me to figure out how to put the cart in reverse. Once we figure it out, we travel backward past the junction and get off the cart to take a closer look at the tracks. There's an old rusty lever that sticks out of a metal box beside the tracks to change direction but it won't move an inch, no matter how hard Beck pulls or kicks at it.

He finally gives up and stomps towards me, his face red and sweaty.

"It's useless! The thing won't budge at all. We're going to have to walk from here."

I chew on my lip trying to think of a way to get the thing to work. We'd come so far in the cart and I wasn't quite ready to give up on it yet. I watch as Glo gets down on her hands and knees to study the switch lever and have an idea.

"What about oil or something to lubricate it? When we pushed the cart out of the building it had been in, the wheels and axles make horrible screeching noises. Abuela had a can of black gunky stuff that she put on it and it ran smoother after that."

He nods his head in agreement. "That might work! It might also help if we had some kind of tool to bang away some of the rust and loosen it."

"OR…we could unlock it?" Glo's voice rings out as she walks towards us.

I look at her in confusion. "What do you mean?"

She stops to brush off her knees and gives me a "duh" look.

"There's a key hole on the side of the box. We need to get the key and unlock it so the lever will move."

I look at Beck but he just shrugs his shoulders so I just ask, "What key?"

A grin splits her face. "The one in the floor where all the buttons are, silly! It's clamped onto the hatch door."

I stare at her for a beat before turning and dashing back to the cart and up the stairs. The panel is already open from when Beck and I figured out how to reverse the wheels and sure enough, there's a key held against it with two tiny brackets. I can't believe I missed it before. I pop it out of its brackets and grab the can of oily sludge from where I had stashed it under the bottom shelf and race back out to where Beck and Glo are standing beside the lever. Beck takes the can from me and pours some of the sludge down into the small opening around the lever. He moves over to the track and studies the lines before pouring more of the slimy stuff on both sides. He hands me the can back and takes the key. The key turns with no problem and the lever moves but Beck has to put a lot of pressure on it to get the switch points on the track to move in the direction we need to go.

Glo's hopping up and down, clapping her hands, so I give her a big smacking kiss on top of her head for solving what will hopefully be our last obstacle before we park the cart. We all get back on and decide to pump instead of using the engine so that we can go slowly and watch for any sign of where my grandfather used to park the cart. The track we had been on before switching had been gradually turning to the south to run parallel to the mountains. This track heads straight for them and the rocks that look like a howling coyote. We keep the speed slow as we get closer and then start to pass the rock formation.

"The tracks are curving ahead!" Glo calls out.

I step to the front windows to get a better look and see the rather sharp turn ahead. "Slower Beck. I can't see where the tracks go around this bend." As we make the turn my eyes go big and I yell, "Brake! Stop, we have to stop!"

Thankfully, we were going slow enough that it was just a small jolt when Beck throws the brakes. He comes and joins us and we all look out dusty, dirty windows at the wall of rock five feet ahead of us.

"Hmmm, I guess this is it then. Who's ready for a hike?" he asks.

Glo yells, "ME" but I just swallow down the knot that's formed in my throat. We made it. We made the first part of the journey but I'm terrified of what we might find at the end of the next one. I take a deep breath and follow them out the door, pulling the hand drawn map from my bag. There should be some kind of pathway or trail to get us started in the right direction but I don't see anything except rock walls on three sides. I look back down at the map and frown at what I see underneath it. The tracks go straight into a smooth rock wall. That makes no sense. Why would anyone run tracks into a wall?

Beck and Glo are unclasping the sled from the trailer and Beck yells for me to come help him get it off, but I'm fixated on the dead-end tracks. I walk the few steps to the wall, reach out and put my hand on it and feel it give slightly. When I pull my hand back, I can see my handprint where dust has come away. I look down at my hand that's now covered in dust and then back at the wall before reaching out and giving it a hard shove. I have to take a quick step back as the whole thing ripples, releasing decades of clinging dust that billows down around me. I move back around the cart to let the dust settle and get Beck and Glo to come see what I've found.

"What is it?" Beck asks when I tell him about what happened.

"I don't know but it's not solid so there's probably something behind it!"

He walks up to it and pushes it a few times seeing the rippling for himself and then drops down to the ground, runs his hand on the steel rail until it connects with the wall and gives a tug on it.

"It's a tarp of some kind! Help me pull it up from the ground."

The three of us start to pull the tarp away from the ground and find long, metal pegs that had been holding it down. Once the bottom is free, we work on the sides of the tarp which were secured to bolts anchored into the real rock walls with some kind of hard plastic bands. Once the whole thing is free except for the top, Beck grabs a corner and drags it to the side, letting the sun shine into the opening.

I move into the space cautiously but I'm surprised to see that it isn't as dark inside as it should be. Looking up, I can see that there is an opening at the top that lets in plenty of light. The space inside is at least twenty feet across and forty feet deep with the tracks stopping towards the end of the space at a small wooden barrier. There are metal shelving units all along one rock wall that hold boxes and piles of tools. I take another spin around and look up at the opening, realizing that my grandfather had created a natural building to store his cart and tools. He had used the natural rock and created doors on either end with the heavy plastic fabric that was the same color as the terrain. It was a perfect way to camouflage his supplies and transportation. I call Beck and Glo inside so they can look around and head to the opposite end of the opening.

The opening at the far end is much smaller than the main opening, maybe around six feet across. I cut away the plastic ties holding it to the wall and kicked out the metal pegs in the ground until I can move the tarp to the side and see what's outside. The back side of Coyote Rock is to my left but on the right is the pathway I have been looking for! I can see it leading up past the rocks and deeper into the mountains. This is the way we will go next.

Beck calls my name from inside so I go back in and join him and Glo who are standing by four blue plastic barrels. Beck has removed the lid on one of them and is peering inside of it. He looks up at me with a grin.

"They're full of water! Not great tasting water, but water!"

I smile back at him and take another look around at the pick axes, shovels and shallow pans that are piled up on the shelves.

"It makes sense. My grandfather would have used this as his staging area to go into the mountains for his mining. I bet if we looked through these boxes we'd find some old food stores too. Probably nothing edible after over thirty years but it's probably here somewhere." I look around again and nod. "Come on, let's get the cart in here and then go through this stuff. We need to decide if we are going to stay here for the rest of the day or start the hike."

Beck nods. "It's got to be almost noon by now. We would be out in the hottest part of the day if we left in the next hour or so. Maybe we should wait and go early tomorrow morning, start when it's a bit cooler. It's going to be hard no matter when we go but being out in the sun all day, we'll have to be very careful and make sure we cover up."

I grab Glo who's scooping water from the open barrel with her hands and letting it flow back in.

"Hey, we might need to drink that stuff! Who wants to drink dirty girl hand water?" I just shake my head at her silly grin. "Come help me bring the cart in. Beck, you hold the tarp back so we don't rip it down."

Glo and I get back on the cart and I release the brakes while Beck pulls the tarp back as far as he can reach. I pump as slow as I can so that we're barely moving. I'm worried that the tarp will catch on the top of the cart and rip down from where it's secured on the top. I'm sure there's a better way to move the tarp but I don't really want to waste any more time figuring it out. I like the idea of having the cart hidden in case Boyd is still after us. Maybe if he doesn't see it, he'll just keep going past us and end up in Mexico.

I sigh in relief when the cart slides into the opening without catching on the tarp and Beck lets it drop down to cover the opening again. I feel safer already. Once I set the brakes, I point Glo towards the supplies on the shelves.

"Give me a hand unloading this stuff. I want to get the sled loaded up so we're ready to go."

I laugh at her when she tries to pull two water jugs from the shelf and they both drop to the cart's floor. I pick them up and use my chin to point at a small box.

"Stick to the lighter things sweetie or you're going to lose a few toes!"

She rolls her eyes at me but does what I say so I carry the jugs off and find Beck wrestling with the sled to get it off the trailer. I drop the jugs and move over to help him. Once the sled is down the three of us work together to load it up with as much as it will hold. If the valley works out then we don't want to have to hike back here anytime soon.

We've just finished up the loading and are about start exploring the boxes my grandfather stored here when the light in the area gets brighter and a voice rings out.

"Hello, brother!"

The massive bang that follows those words has Glo and me screaming and ducking.

Chapter Twenty-Six

The punishing sun beams down on Boyd and even the little bit of breeze created by the buggy's speed does nothing to help the nausea and dizziness he feels. He consumed the last of the food and water the night before and he knows if he doesn't find his brother and the girl today, he will likely be dead by tomorrow.

He squints his eyes behind his goggles for any sight of them in the distance but doesn't see anything except a large rock formation beside the tracks he's following. He grits his teeth in frustration as the rocks go by and a flap of his scarf blows up into his face. He tosses his head to the side to move the scarf and it's that movement that lets him see a bit of the cart tucked around the side of the rocks he's passing.

He slams on the brakes and reverses quickly so that the buggy is hidden back behind the rocks and then takes a deep breath. This is it. This is the moment when he will finally get everything he deserves. He gets out of the buggy and quietly closes the door, then checks the load in his gun. There are exactly three bullets left after the shootout at the bridge but that's all he'll need to take care of his coward of a brother and the two girls.

He edges around the rocks and leans out to look over the cart he's been chasing for three days but pulls back quickly when he catches a glimpse of all three of his prey. The two girls are climbing onto the cart but he doesn't see what his brother's doing so he just waits for a few minutes and then peeks around the rocks again. The cart, the girls, and his brother are nowhere in sight so he edges around into the open and stares in confusion at the space where they were a few minutes ago. He walks along the tracks up to what looks like a blank wall of rock and reaches out. Just as his hand is about to touch the rock he hears a faint voice.

"Give me a hand unloading this stuff. I want to get the sled loaded up so we're ready to go."

The girl's voice is coming from the other side of the wall so he pushes his hand against it and grins when it gives. Clever, not rock but a tarp that looks like its rock. He edges to the side and finds the end of it so he can peek past it and see what's on the other side. He sees some kind of dim cavern but he can make out the cart and the three of them loading up supplies on a platform that is resting on the ground. He decides to let them finish loading it before he makes his move. They must be going to wherever the gold is so he'll need those supplies. He gives them five more minutes to get the work done and then pulls the tarp violently to the side and rushes through into the cavern with his gun up. His eyes zero in on Beck with hate and he forgets his vow not to kill his only family.

"Hello, brother!"

He grins with satisfaction when he sees Beck's eyes widen in fear a split second before he pulls the trigger. The bullet hits the mark and Beck spins around with the force of it then crashes down to the ground where his head smashes against the steel track and he goes deathly still.

He turns to see the girls have dropped to the ground and he smirks in amusement when he sees that Claudia had thrown herself on top of the little one. He can use that protectiveness to get what he wants.

"Shut up! Stop that screaming right now!" He bellows at them when the echoes of the noise they're making cause his head to throb.

He strides over and grabs Claudia's arm and hauls her away from the small girl under her.

"Get up!" He yells at her and then snaps his fingers in front of her eyes to get her to focus on him instead of the still form of his brother. "I'm going to put a bullet in your sister's head if you don't do exactly what I say."

That does the trick as her terrified eyes lock in on his face so he nods and pushes her away and then hauls the small girl up by her scrawny arm. He wraps his arm around her from behind and pulls her against him so he can position the barrel of his gun against her temple.

"Here's the deal, you do what I say, you give me what I want and I will let the kid live. You give me a hard time or try anything then I start putting holes in her. You'd be surprised how long a person can live with a few holes in them so watch yourself!"

Claudia's eyes had lost some of the terror as she looked frantically between her now sobbing sister and the pool of blood that's forming around Beck so Boyd barks at her, "Never mind him. He's dead. He can't help you now! If you don't want your sister to join him then you better give me what I want!"

She nods her head slowly and asks, "What is it? What do you want from us?"

A grin spreads across his face. "First off, water. I want lots of water and something to eat. After that, you can hand over the gold!"

Chapter Twenty-Seven

I have no idea what he's talking about! Gold? What gold? This idiot just chased us across hundreds of miles for something I don't have? Beck's dead or he soon will be if I can't get to him and Glo's life rests on me giving this monster something I have no way of getting. My expression must show my thoughts because he scowls and pushes the gun harder against Glo's head causing her to let out a shriek of pain and terror.

"Don't even think about messing with me, girl! I know your gramps use to mine these hills for gold and you were coming here to get his stash to pay your way over the wall. Well, now it's going to be my ticket over! Call it payment for the injury and trouble you've caused me."

I open my mouth to deny it but the fanatical look in his eyes tells me he won't believe any denial I can say so I just let out a breath and nod. The only way I can see out of this is to play along and wait for my chance to somehow either get the gun away from him or shoot him with my own. His next words take one of those options away.

"You can hand over that gun you shot me with too. You didn't think I'd forgotten about that, did you? I owe you some payback just for that alone!"

I curse under my breath but slowly pull the gun out of my bag and drop it on the sandy ground of the cavern before kicking it past him closer to where Beck's laying on the ground. Hopefully, he's playing possum and can help us but he doesn't even flinch when sand from where the gun lands sprays up into his face.

Boyd scowls at me and gives Glo a hard shake to punish me. "Real cute, girl, but he's not going to be able to help you. Now go and get me one of those jugs of water and something to eat! After that, I want to hear about the gold."

I hold up my hands and start backing away to hopefully calm him down a bit so he won't terrorize Glo more than he already is. I wrack my brain for a convincing lie about the gold I don't have. If I can't sell him on it, I know he'll just kill both of us. I grab a jug of water and the basket of food I had prepared that morning for our hike to the valley and bring it back to him. I set them down a few feet from him and take a few steps back when he waves me further away.

He shoves Glo to the ground and lowers himself down beside her, keeping the gun pointed at her side across his body. His finger never leaves the trigger as he reaches out and pulls the water jug towards him, using one hand to flip the cap off before guzzling down a bit of it. I stand there waiting while he eats and drinks his fill. My eyes keep tracking between the deathly still Beck and the barrel of the gun pointed at my sister. I can't bear to meet her eyes because I know I won't be able to stand by and do nothing if I see just how scared she is. I need to be smart about this and play along with this psycho until the right opportunity presents itself for me to make my move. It's one of the hardest things I've ever done because all I want to do right now is launch myself at this monster and bash his head in. Instead, I force myself to take a few deep breaths and tune out her heartbreaking sobs and whimpers.

Once he's done eating and drinking, he tosses the empty jug across the cavern where it bounces off the cart and falls to the sand, then raises his eyebrows at me so I start spinning a tale I hope he buys.

"The gold's not here. That's why we were loading up the sled with supplies. We have to hike two days into the mountains to get to where my grandfather stashed it."

His eyes narrow in suspicion before he takes another look at the loaded sled and then slowly nods and pushes himself to his feet, pulling Glo up with him.

"Alrighty then! Let's get going."

I shake my head in protest, trying to stall. "That's not a good idea. We can't hike right now during the hottest part of the day."

He gives me a dead stare before shoving Glo forward.

"Nice try. We just traveled across an entire desert in the sun. A little hike won't kill us." A small smirk forms on his face. "Well, it won't kill me. Not sure if both of you will make it, though!" The amusement leaves his face and he waves the gun towards the sled. "Start hauling that thing, we're leaving right now and if you try anything…anything…the kid is dead. I don't need her to make you do what I want. There's plenty of ways I could persuade you without her."

I stare into his empty eyes and know he won't have a problem killing a little girl and then torturing me for what he wants. All traces of humanity are gone from this monster and when he's done with us there won't be any negotiating for our lives. He'll discard us like useless garbage and never give it another thought. This realization should steal all hope from me but instead, it just firms my resolve to kill him at the first possible opportunity, so I just nod my head at him.

I need the sled remote that I had stuffed into my back pocket so I tell him what I'm reaching for. He just looks confused so I slowly reach back and pull it out. I take a look around the cavern one more time, my eyes glancing off Beck's body and force the pain and grief of his death down deep. I silently vow to avenge him. He didn't deserve this, none of us do. I shift my focus to Glo. If we are going to be out in the full afternoon sun then there are precautions that need to be taken so I make my case to Boyd.

"If you want us to last for more than an hour out there, then we'll need our scarves and goggles to protect us from the sun. They're in the cart. Can I get them and cover her up before we leave?"

He just waves his gun towards the cart in an impatient motion for me to hurry up so I spin around and bound up the steps into the cart. My eyes fly over every surface looking for some kind of weapon I can use but we've loaded everything on to the sled already and I gave our one knife to Beck to use after I cut the ties holding the tarp to the rock wall. The only thing left inside here are our scarves and goggles so I grab them into a bundle, climb back down and step over to the sled hoping to grab something I can use.

Boyd barks out, "Get the girl covered and let's go! No more stalling!" Before he shoves her in my direction.

I catch her in my arms and pull her against me for a brief moment of comfort and then gently push her away so I can arrange the scarves around her head after I put her goggles around her neck. It's a pathetic amount of protection for her against the cruel midday sun but it's the best we have.

I lean down and kiss her forehead and barely whisper, "I'm going to save us, I promise."

Her eyes are just rising to meet mine when she's wrenched out of my arms by Boyd. He points his gun at me and then at the sled before whirling it around in a let's go motion. I glare at him but just nod before draping my own scarves over my head and then turning the sled on. The noise startles Boyd making him turn the gun back on me again.

"What the hell is that?" He almost screams as he looks frantically around for the source of the low humming.

I throw up my hands with the remote in one of them. "Whoa, whoa! It's just the hover sled!"

I can see by the confusion in his eyes that he doesn't know what a hover sled is so I try and reassure him that I'm not trying anything.

"There's an engine on the sled that lifts it so we don't have to carry or drag it. That's what the remote controls."

He shakes his head and grits his teeth. "Whatever, just get going!"

I nod and use the remote to send the sled towards the back of the cavern, past Beck's body. I try and get a closer look at him as I go by and see that he has two pools of blood under him. There's the one where he was shot and one from a gash on the side of his head. Any hope I have of him being ok vanishes when I see the second wound. If he's not dead already, he will be soon with no one to help him. I try and see if his chest is rising and falling but I get a hard shove to the back from Boyd that sends me stumbling away. I have to shove the tears and sorrow over Beck's loss down deep for now and concentrate on what I'm doing so if a chance opens to defeat Boyd, I'll be ready.

I step ahead of the sled so I can pull the tarp aside and send it through into the glare of the sun. Boyd shoves Glo through and waves for me to go so I won't be behind him. I don't even get a last glance at Beck because he's blocking my view of him. I have no choice but to say a silent goodbye and send a mental apology for all the pain he's had to go through because of his despicable brother as I turn and leave my only friend for good. I pull my focus to the path ahead and square my shoulders. I'm ready for what comes and I'll take my chance at taking Boyd out as soon as it happens.

Glo's waiting beside the sled at the bottom of the path so I nod at her to start up with the sled following behind her. I'm relieved at the space between her and Boyd and his gun. If I see a spot in the path ahead to send her away, she might be able to hide and circle back to the cart. It only takes Boyd ten minutes to come to the same conclusion causing him to rearrange our order so I'm in front with the sled and Glo's back with him. I fume in frustration as I trudge along beside the sled. The path takes us up higher and I can feel the burn in my thighs as the sweat rolls down into my eyes and soaks through my shirt on my back. The only thing I can be grateful about is the silence. Other than a few grunts, I haven't had to listen to any taunts or threats from Boyd. Maybe we'll get lucky and he'll keel over with heat exhaustion and die. He can't be used to this kind of exertion in the high heat either.

Just as the thought of that runs through my mind, I flinch when his arm shoots past me to snag one of our jugs of water. He doesn't say anything when I grab one of my own and drop back to make Glo drink. We don't speak but her eyes are filled with all the questions she wants to ask me about what we're going to do to get out of this. All I can do is give her a reassuring smile before Boyd shoves me back to the front with the sled. I take a few deep swallows of water from the jug before capping it and setting it back on the sled. Just because Boyd's hijacked our hike doesn't mean we don't have to ration the water. Especially now that he's chugging away at his bottle like we have an unlimited supply. Glo and I **will** make it to the valley but as soon as I find a way to get rid of Boyd, I'm going straight back to the cavern to check and see if Beck's still alive. I can't just leave him there without knowing for sure. I gave up on him once, a long time ago. I won't do it again.

Chapter Twenty-Eight

Pain, blinding pain, in my head that has my stomach heaving, causing me to roll to my side and expel the meager contents of my stomach. A different shriek of agonizing pain flares from the side of my body. I try and push myself up from the sand but the world blurs and spins, sending me face first back into the ground. Dark wings threaten the sides of my vision and all I want to do is escape into the dark where I won't feel this agony but an image of my brother's cruel face keeps me in the here and now. Boyd did this to me so that means the girls are in danger. A surge of urgency floods through me so I channel all my strength into my arms to push myself up off of the ground. I whip my head around looking for them but the motion to my damaged head has me toppling back to the ground and darkness overtakes me once again.

The next time I come too, the light in the cavern is much dimmer. I take it slower this time and gradually get to a sitting position. The pain is still flaring strong in my side and my head so I just sit and slowly look around the cavern to try and figure out what happened. I'm alone and the sled is missing so I have to assume that the girls are still alive somewhere out there with Boyd. The urgency to run after them floods through me but I know I won't make it two steps in my condition. I raise my hand and gently probe the large bump and gash on the side of my head. Even the softest pressure on it sends a spike of pain and my stomach threatens to heave again. My hand comes away wet with blood but it's sticky like it's old blood that's started to dry, so I move on to the injury on my side.

My whole shirt is soaked with blood on that side and I wince when I peel it away from the wound. I can't get a good look at the injury so I use my fingers again to try and judge the damage. My head swoons again when one of my fingers almost slides into a hole that shouldn't be there. I take a few minutes of deep breathing before I get the courage up to feel along my side to the back and find another hole. The bullet has gone straight through me and judging from the location and my limited knowledge of anatomy, it's not life threatening except for the blood that keeps leaking out of me. Both the front and back wounds are caked with sand from the ground and I don't know for sure but I think it's the sand that slowed the bleeding down and kept me from dying while I was unconscious. I don't know if that's true or not but I do know that I need to clean the wounds out or I will be dead from infection and it's going to hurt …a lot.

I look around the cavern again and think about what I need to do first. I'm going to need water to clean out the wounds and some kind of bandages to close them up. My mouth is as dry as the sand I'm sitting on so I'm definitely dehydrated too. I zero in on the old barrels of water and decide that's my first step, but actual stepping isn't an option yet so I just crawl on hands and knees toward it. I only make it a few feet before my knee comes down on something hard, adding another blast of pain to my abused body. When I pull back and to see what caused it, I'm grateful for this pain. Día's gun is half buried in the sand where my knee pushed it. It doesn't help me right now but once I'm back on my feet and can go after them, it might give me the edge I need to finish the threat that my brother is. I leave it in place for now and make my way to the barrels, first things first.

I use the rim to pull myself up to my feet for the first time and hold tight and grit my teeth as the cavern spins around me. Once things settle again, I scoop up hand after hand of water and drink my fill. I'm grateful that the water seems to push the pain in my head back and my legs feel steadier already. I spend the next few minutes staggering around the cavern going through the bins that are stacked on the shelves - looking for any supplies that I can use to treat my wounds. I bark out a groan of relief when I pry open one of the plastic lids of a bin and see that it's filled with white metal boxes with a red cross stamped on the lids. I pull each one out and set them on the shelf beside the bin until I count six in total. The relief that fills me is only temporary because I know how much it's going to hurt to treat my wounds. I gather three of the boxes from the shelf and carry them to the tarp at the opening and slide through into to the brighter light where I'll be able to see what I'm doing. I can get a better feel of what time it is now that I can see where the sun is in the sky and let out a breath. It's not as late as I thought it was. It was only around noon when we were loading the sled and judging by the sun, it's now mid-afternoon. That means at most, Boyd and the girls are only a few hours ahead of me.

I dump the med boxes on the sand and stagger back into the cavern. I grab two empty buckets from the mining supplies and fill them up from the barrels of water to take outside with me but only take a few steps before I'm forced to set them down. The gunshot wound on my left side has turned into a screaming demon from lifting the bucket and all the strength in my arm on that side is gone. It takes me way longer than it should to shuffle each bucket of water out into the sun one at a time using only my good arm. I finally drop to the sand coated in sweat, my head and stomach spinning with a fresh bloom of blood soaking my side.

I spend a few minutes just getting my energy back and sipping handfuls of water from one of the buckets until I'm ready to get started. I brace myself and pull my shirt over my head and then toss it into one of the buckets to rinse off as much of the blood and sweat as I can. While it soaks, I start opening the med kits. At first, I'm thrilled at the stack of paper covered bandages and foil packages that fill it but as soon as I try and pick up the paper covered ones, they just crumble in my hand into brittle pieces. Age and the dry hot air have turned them into barely held together dust. I empty the box of everything wrapped in paper and hold my breath as I tear open the first of four foil packets. The first one holds a set of steel tools, small scissors, a wicked sharp scalpel, tweezers, and a needle with a loop of thread attached in a tiny plastic bag. The second foil pouch holds a roll of pink stretchy fabric that's held closed with metal clasps. The third packet's contents make me close my eyes in thanks. The label states that it's a quick-clot sponge. I don't know if the chemical components will still work after all these years but I can at least pack the two holes with it.

The final foil pouch holds a rock-hard biscuit of some kind. I turn the foil packaging over and the words "ER Bar - High-calorie ration bar" are on the faded label. I'm guessing it's some kind of food so I put it back in the foil and set it to the side before checking the box for anything that's left. There's a small tube of ointment that is completely dried up and a tiny aerosol can with the words 'Wound Wash' on it. My breath catches at those words. It's going to hurt but I need to get the holes as clean and free of sand as I can so I swallow down the trepidation.

I go grab the other four kits from the shelf inside and lay out everything I'm going to need to get this done. I wring out my gross shirt as best as I can and dip it in the clean bucket of water before using it to wipe away as much of the blood and sand on my head and side as I can. It hurts so bad that tears constantly pour down my face and painful grunts come from my lips but I keep at it until the water in both buckets is red from my blood. I use the spray from all six cans and yelp out my misery as it burns in the wounds. I can't stop now even though I want to flop down on the sand and just die. The quick clot sponges come next and I use the pink elastic roll to secure them in place. I must look like a fool with the one wrapped around my forehead but no one's around to see so I don't care.

I wish I could jump up and go chase after the girls but I'm going to have to just sit here for a while and recover from the trauma I just inflicted on my body. I lean back against the warm rock wall and watch as the sun drops further down until my eye lids follow it and close. My last thought before I slip away is, I hope my friends are ok.

Chapter Twenty-Nine

We've only been hiking for a few hours in the hot sun when I hear Glo stumble behind me. I turn to look and see Boyd haul her back up and shove her forward so I just try and send her a reassuring smile but I know it comes out flat. It's only a few minutes later that I hear her let out a small gasp and then the sound of her hitting the ground. I whirl around and yell at him as I rush to lift her back up.

"Don't touch her!"

He glares at me and stabs the gun in our direction. "I don't need her to get what I want from you so she either keeps up or I get rid of her! She's just slowing us down anyway so…"

He leaves that threatening sentence open for me to fill in the blanks. I'm going to have to carry her or he'll do something drastic. I turn around and squat down so she can climb onto my back when my eyes land on the sled. I stand back up, take her arm and pull her ahead to it. It only takes a few seconds to move our supplies around so there's a spot for her to sit in the middle of the sled. The kid can't weigh more than seventy-five pounds so it's shouldn't have any problems with her extra weight on it. I take a minute to dry her tears and then help her step up and get settled onto the sled and then hand her one of our battered umbrellas to open up and use for shade. She gives me a shaky nod that she is ok but I know she's far from it. In the last three days, this poor girl's whole world has come crumbling down around her. She's lost her home, her grandmother, her friend Beck, and now faces death by this evil man. I know she's going to have emotional scars for a very long time. I just hope we can live through this so we can work on healing them.

Boyd interrupts my musings. "Well, look at the queen of the desert riding on her throne!" He says sarcastically. "Now that just doesn't seem fair, does it? I think maybe the man with the gun should be the one riding in style. Don't you?"

I bite my tongue to keep the nasty reply I want to bark back at him in and take a deep breath before answering.

"I'm not sure if it could handle your weight. Even if it could, the charge wouldn't last as long and we'd have to stop often to power it back up. Glo's weight shouldn't affect it that much but we can try with you on it if you want."

He stares at me suspiciously for a few seconds before finally shaking his head.

"Maybe later. Let's get moving! We've wasted enough time."

I turn without a word and get the sled moving again up the path ahead of me. So far, it's been wide enough that I can walk beside it but I'm worried about what's ahead. I had taken a good long look at the first part of the map before Boyd showed up but I know I'm going to have to look at it again soon to make sure we stay on track. I'm afraid if he sees the map, he'll take it and start asking questions about the different paths marked on it. Two of the paths marked on the map lead to my Grandfather's mining claims where he made his fortune and the other one leads to the valley. There's no way I'm going to lead Boyd to the valley. He wants gold so I'll take him to one of the claims and he can pry it from the rock with his bare hands for all I care. Hopefully, somewhere between here and there I'll get my opening to either escape with Glo or kill him.

We are moving faster now that Glo isn't setting the pace but it doesn't take very long for Boyd to start slowing us down again. Poor guy, he's not used to exerting himself outside in the full heat of the day. He calls for me to slow down a few times as a gap grows between us but I only slow down for a few minutes at a time before speeding back up. A little bit of distance between us is a good thing for me. As the path goes around a rock outcropping I take the few seconds that I'm out of his sight to pull the map from my bag and scan it for what's ahead. There's a split in the path ahead that will take us in the direction I want to go and even better, it looks like it will climb a hill. I want Boyd to be as exhausted as possible so I will have an edge on him.

"Hey! I said, slow down! It's not a race so quit running!"

I can hear him huffing and puffing as he gets closer so I stuff the map back into my bag and turn with an innocent expression.

"I'm sorry, Boyd. I just thought you'd want to get there as quick as possible. You said my sister was slowing us down so now that she's not, I just assumed you wanted to go quicker."

He comes to a stop in front of me with his chest heaving and his breath coming out like a bellows and just scowls at me. I'm just about to turn around and keep going when out of the blue he hauls off and slams his hand against the side of my head, sending me flying into the sled. Glo lets out a squawk of surprise when the sled jerks to the side and crashes into the rock wall we were going around.

I'm half draped over the sled with the hard boxes and jugs digging into my stomach and my knees stinging from landing on the unforgiving rock we are walking on as I try and blink the stars from my reeling head. I can hear Glo crying again and I want to reassure her but all that comes out of my mouth is a groan. I swallow hard and go to try and get to my feet again when I feel Boyd grab a handful of shirt from my back and haul me back up and on to my feet. He grips my arm hard when I sway and gives me a little shake.

"I think we need to clear up how this works. I tell YOU what to do. You obey! I'm getting tired of your mouth so from now on you keep your trap shut. Got it?" He gives me another shake to emphasize his point and I feel my head bob up and down at his shaking. Thankfully, he takes that as my agreement and lets me go. He stabs a finger past me and motions for me to get moving so I slowly turn and start walking. The sled seems to be ok after its crash with the rubber bumpers doing their job. I meet Glo's eyes but look away quickly when I see the hopelessness in them. She doesn't believe we're going to get out of this but she's wrong. I'm going to kill that bastard the first opportunity I get.

The next few hours are spent in silence except for the scuff of our feet over the rocky terrain. I've zoned out as the burn in my thighs from the uphill climb matches the burn of the sun beating down on my scarf wrapped head. I stumble without warning when the land levels out for the first time in what feels like hours and look up to take in what's ahead. We've reached a saddle clearing between two giant rock peaks that runs for about four hundred feet before dropping away. As happy as I am to be walking on flat ground again, I'm also nervous because I can see at least five fissures in the ground ahead that we will have to jump over. The first few look like they're only a couple of feet across and should be manageable but the third is a dark gap in the rock that from here looks at least four or five feet across. I've paused as I try and work out how the sled is going to go over it but shake my head. It must be doable if my grandfather traveled this route to his claim. My next thought is how I can use the large fissure to my advantage. If I can time it right, I might be able to catch Boyd off guard and shove him down into it.

"What's the holdup?" Boyd gasps from behind me so I move to the side and just point out what's ahead.

He takes his time looking around to catch his breath and guzzle down way too much water. I look away to hide my disgust when he finishes off his second jug of the hike and tosses the empty container on the ground. The way he's not even trying to ration tells me again that he doesn't care that there won't be enough left to support all three of us for more than a few days. He's just going to kill us and take it all for himself.

Glo's grunt of surprise has me spinning back around. Boyd's dragged her from her spot on the sled and has her clutched against him.

"You first, with the sled. Once you're across, we'll follow."

I try and keep the glare from my eyes when I realize I won't be pushing him into a crack after all. Instead, I just turn and get the sled moving. It's an easy hop over the first two cracks and when I get to the third I see it's only about six feet deep and four feet across so it wouldn't have been deep enough to cause him much damage anyway, even if I could have pushed him into it. There's no way I can guide the sled over it though. With nothing for the air to push against, it would just tip right in so I spend some time going back and forth along the crack until I find my grandfather's work. Butted up against one of the rock walls that hem in the area is a section of six planks that span the crack. The planks look like wood but when I get down and push on them to see if they are rotted it turns out that they are some kind of hard plastic that just resembles wood. It seems sturdy enough so I take a tentative step out on them and let out a breath of relief when there's no give.

Once the sled is across, I move back to the center of the saddle and turn and wave Boyd forward, pointing to where I crossed. The shadows from the peaks are making it harder to see the ground ahead but the last few fissures are no more than two feet across so I make my way to the end and look down on what's next. The land drops down at a steep angle before climbing back up between another set of peaks. I turn and look up at the sky. There's at most another hour of decent light left. I don't want to even think about navigating that descent and climb in the dark. Also, the humming from the sled is becoming more sluggish so I think the battery is winding down. I bite my lip and try and find the right words to tell Boyd that we have to stop for the day without him lashing out at me again as he catches up. Thankfully, he's not a total idiot and when he sees what comes next he just points to the ground with a grunt.

"We stop here for the night. Get me some food!"

He'd pushed Glo to the ground when he caught up so I take a second to smooth the scarves back from her hair and face and bend down to plant a kiss on her forehead. My heart aches when she doesn't even raise her eyes to meet mine but just keeps them fixed on the ground in front of her. She's given up and shutting down. There's nothing I can say to her to make it better with Boyd steps away so I just sigh and head over to the sled.

He follows me and while I pull the basket that I put the food I made earlier in and rummages through all the supplies. When he grabs yet another jug of water I take a few steps away so I'm not in hitting range and say, "That's all the water we have. There's nowhere to replace it ahead."

The jug is halfway to his lips when he lowers it with a nasty look my way before taking in the other jugs still on the sled.

"Looks like there's plenty to me." He says sarcastically.

I shake my head and take another step back. "We still have a day and a half of hiking then the return trip to the cavern and then back to town, if that's where you're going. It won't last if we don't ration it."

He doesn't dispute me, just glowers at me before lifting the jug to his lips. I don't show my satisfaction when I see he only takes a swallow before capping it back up. He drops the jug back on the sled and points to the basket.

"What's in there?"

I hold it out to him at arm's reach bracing myself for a hit from him but he just snatches it from me and pulls out more food than he should for one meal then drops it to the ground in front of me. When he walks away and settles on the ground, I turn to the sled, start opening the bumpers and fanning out the solar panels to catch the last light of the day. After that, I grab the basket and settle down beside Glo and pull her into my lap. I hand her some food and we eat quickly. I watch Boyd out of the corner of my eye as he finishes his meal and starts to relax. I can see his eyelids are looking heavy and I might have a shot of just running with Glo if he falls asleep.

I give it a few more minutes and start plotting. Slide Glo off my lap and rise to our feet. Snatch a jug of water and bolt down the slope in front of us, find somewhere to hide in the dark. We can't go back because it's wide open and he can just shoot us as we run so even though I don't want to go down that steep slope in the dark, it's our only option.

I glance his way again and see his eyes have closed completely. This is it, this is our chance. I tense up to move just as Glo lets out a croak from a dry throat.

"Can I have some water?"

Boyd's eyes pop open with a jerk and he scrambles to his feet. The gun's pointed at us again causing me to drop my head in frustration as he motions me to my feet. I slide Glo off of my lap and push myself up to face him.

"Get the kid a drink then bring that rope I saw on the sled over here."

I shuffle over to the sled in defeat. He's going to tie us up for the night. There's nothing I can do now so I grab the rope and a jug of water as exhaustion sets in. All the adrenaline that has been keeping me going is starting to recede, leaving me feeling weak. I toss the rope toward him and help Glo drink from the heavy jug before taking my own drink. As soon as we're done, Boyd waves Glo over to him and wraps the thick nylon rope we had found in with the mining supplies around her waist and then ties a loop of it around his own, leaving four feet of slack in between them. He grabs my arm and spins me around before dropping down behind me and looping the rope between my legs until there's less than a foot between my feet, effectively hobbling me. He finishes off by wrapping another loop around my waist and then attaching it to his waist. Now both Glo and I are bound to him and won't be going anywhere in the night without him feeling it. He shoves us both in different directions away from each other and drops to the ground, dragging us down with him.

"Go to sleep!" He mutters as he lays down.

I rub at my sore tailbone that I landed on when he yanked the rope and look over at Glo who has curled up in a small ball facing away from me. I can see her shoulders shaking as she cries silently causing my anger to override my caution.

"At least let me sleep with her!" I rage at him.

He cracks one eye briefly before shutting it again. "Just be grateful I'm tired and want to sleep, girl. You and me are due for a...conversation...and it won't be about sleeping with your sister. Now shut up and go to sleep or I might find the energy to have that talk tonight!"

A cold shiver runs down my back. I know exactly what he's implying. I'd rather die first! With one last look at Glo in the fading light, I lower myself down to the unforgiving rock and close my eyes. I think about tomorrow. I think about the valley that's so close but also so far away now and I think about Beck. Then I let my own silent tears flow.

Chapter Thirty

I wake up to a dull ache coming from both my side and head with the full moon beaming down on me like a spotlight. My butt is numb and my neck is locked stiff from falling asleep leaning back against the rock so it takes me a few minutes of rolling my head around to loosen it up. I gently touch the bandages on both the front and back of my side but I can't feel any dampness so I guess the bleeding has stopped, for now. That might change because there are things I need to do, I've rested enough.

I use the wall to pull myself up and am pleased that my head doesn't swim the way it had earlier. I dump out the bloody water from both buckets and put the med kits in them to carry back inside so I don't have to make as many trips. A flare of pain wells up in my side when I use that arm to pick up one of the buckets but it's not the white-hot spear that it was earlier. I don't try and fool myself that I'm on the mend, I know that it'll take days of no activity for that. But that's not an option for me. My friends are out there somewhere in danger and I'm going to find them and save them. Even if it kills me.

I'm happy to see that there's full moonlight filling the cavern so I make use of it before it fades away. I find one of the shallow pans from the mining equipment and after rinsing the dust from it, fill it with clean water and put three of the rock-hard ration bars from the med kits in it to soak and hopefully soften. I don't know if there's any calories in those bars after so many years but my stomach needs something in it so I'll be eating them as soon as they won't break my teeth.

Before Boyd showed up, we had taken a quick look at what was on the shelves but we hadn't really opened everything to see what all was there. I do remember seeing two black bags with straps on one of the shelves so I pull them off but have to let them drop to the ground when the surprising weight of them is too much for my wounded side to bear. I end up just dragging them one at a time to the middle of the cavern, where there is the most light, and start emptying them of what's inside and sorting it into piles. I can't stop grinning when I end up with two complete changes of clothes. All I own is the clothes on my back, consisting of the stiff with dirt and blood pants that I'm wearing and a shirt that's now nothing but a bloody rag after I used it to clean my wounds. My socks and underwear, well, they are beyond salvageable at this point. Having a fresh set of clothes is almost as good as finding food.

There's a smaller version of the medical boxes I had found earlier but this one has a sealed bottle of painkillers in it. I hold that bottle in my hand and stare at it for a moment in thought. What are the chances that after all these years they would have any effective properties to them? I decide I don't care so I peel the wrapper away and chew all six of the bitter white pills and hope they don't kill me.

I find a coil of rope and a roll of plastic wrapped silver tape that I set aside. The last three things in the main compartment of the bag are foil pouches with MRE stamped on the side and a wind-up flashlight. I have no idea what an MRE is so I spend a few minutes winding the light up with my good arm until I get a weak beam from it and use it to read the fine print on the foil pouches. When I get the gist of what Meal Ready to Eat is, my eyes go wide and swing them over to the pan of hard bars sitting in water that was going to be my next meal before shaking my head with a smile. Looks like I'll be eating slightly better after all.

I take my time following the directions on the package and marvel at how easily it heats up as a slight smell of spicy tomatoes fills the air. There are more pockets on the outside of the pack and a weird container built into the side of it that has rubber tubing attached to it. I find a compass and a folding knife in one pocket and a dozen thin foil packets the length and width of my finger in the other. The packets are orange, blue and green and have the words Gator-Ade on them. They feel squishy when I squeeze them but I can't tell what's in them so I just tear one open, sending orange dust everywhere. I sniff at the open foil, surprised at the faint fruity smell so I tentatively lick at some of the orange dust on my hand. It tastes vaguely like oranges but sort of salty too.

The light goes out before I can look more closely at the packaging so I have to spend more time cranking it. The moon has moved further across the sky so the cavern now has no natural light to help me see. I spend a while just sitting in the dark cranking at the light so it will last longer this time. I place it on one of the shelves to shine directly on the area I'm working in and leave both my hands free. I finally figure out that the colored powder is added to water to give it flavor and after looking closer at the pack and container with the tube, realize that it's a built-in canteen.

I sit and eat the first hot meal I've had in days and think about what comes next. Mainly, find my friends and end my brother. Thanks to Día's grandfather, I have everything I need here to survive on the hike. The only question that remains is if my body will let me get it done. I take stock of my injuries thoughtfully. I don't know if there was something left in those pills I chewed or if it's the hot food filling my belly but I feel a million times better. My side still hurts but not as severely as it did earlier and my headache is almost gone. I want to leave well enough alone but I know I have to change my bandages and secure it better. The pink stretchy fabric won't hold up once I really start moving.

I finish my meal and get to work on the bandages while I'm feeling better. I use the silver tape to bind it in place and push all thoughts of the pain it will cause when I will have to pull it off of my skin in the future from my mind. Once that's done, I do the same to the gash on my head with a smaller piece of tape and hope it will stay in place once I start sweating. I change into the fresh clothes and put the second set in the bottom of the pack I had emptied. The other pack I pulled off the shelf was a duplicate to the first one so I consolidated everything I wanted to take into one and leave the rest of the supplies on the shelves for if we ever come back here. The pack I want to take with me contains a set of clothes with an extra pair of underwear and socks, three MRE's, the extra flashlight, compass, knife and all the drink powders from both bags. The final item I need to take is one med kit with all the useable sponges, sprays and pills I can jam into it.

I close it all up, take a deep breath and lift it. It's heavy but not as heavy as it was before with the rope and large roll of tape in it. The problem is water. I haven't filled the container up yet so that will make it even heavier, and judging by the size of it, it won't be enough. Once the sun is up and I'm hiking, I'll need more than just that one container if it takes me more than a few days to find Día and Glo. I go back to the other pack and figure out how to release the container from it and discard the tubing so it will stay sealed and then fill both containers up, add the flavored powder and put the spare in the pack. I lift it again and feel the burn in my side as it pulls at the wounds. I have to put this pack on my back and carry it all while hiking with a bullet wound in my side. That thought reminds me of the most important thing I need to take, the gun.

I lower the pack back to the ground and go pull the gun from the sand where I left it, then go sit down with the bag and look over the straps. There's the two that go over my shoulders and then two others that go across my body. One set encircles my chest under my arms and the other goes around my waist to let my hips take some of the weight. It's the lower ones that worry me. Once they're clipped closed the straps will only be a few inches under the wound and if they move around could rub right against the bandages causing both a huge amount of pain and the wound to start bleeding again.

The other option I see is to use the rope to make a harness of some sort and drag the stupid thing behind me but that will bring its own set of problems. The only way to know if it's going to be possible is to put it on and see if it will work. I'm not going to let this stop me from going after my friends so I might as well just do it.

I swing around on my bottom until my back is to the pack and maneuver my arms through the straps while its weight is resting on the ground and then clip the belts around me and tighten the straps until they're snug. I clench my jaw against the pain I know is coming and lean forward until the pack is all the way off the ground and on my back. Then I use the shelves to pull myself to my feet and stand, stuff the gun in my pocket and just stand there sweating as I get used to the weight and the pain it has caused. I don't move as I force myself to picture Claudia and Gloria's faces, cowering in fear of my brother, until I feel the rage overtake me. I snatch the flashlight from the shelf where I left it to shine and head towards the tarp covering the opening that leads to the path. When I get past the tarp I shine the light on the ground until I see the path and look up and to the East where the beginnings of false dawn are starting to lighten the sky. I put my head down and step onto the path. I'm going to get my friends.

Chapter Thirty-One

If there's a stronger word for hate then that's how I feel about Boyd. Loathe, despise, scorn, none of those words are strong enough to express just how much I hate him. There isn't a shred of human decency left in this man and I truly believe that killing him would be doing the whole world a favor. I never thought I was a violent person before but now I plot different ways to kill him with every step I take as I struggle to climb this steep slope. These dark thoughts help fuel the rage that's giving me the will to make it up the difficult ascent while pulling a flagging Glo with me. He taunts us to move faster from his royal perch on the hover sled that he's been lounging on since we started this morning.

He woke us by jerking the ropes he'd tied us with until we both came sputtering awake, laughing gleefully when Gloria let out a small scream of shock. He untied my feet and the rope that connected both of us to him, but then tied Glo and me together with only a few feet of slack between us so we were forced to stay side by side. He didn't even have the decency to look away as we did our bathroom business. I had thought going in a bowl in the cart with Beck was embarrassing, but this was flat out humiliating as he watched us with a wicked sneer.

Once we had finished our business he lost interest and stomped over to the sled to grab the basket of food. There wasn't much left in it after he plowed through it the night before so he threw it to the ground after eating what was left.

"Looks like no breakfast for you two! Oh well, time to eat the miles." He said with a cruel laugh.

I shook my head in disbelief. Did this idiot really think we could hike all day with no food in us?

"The sled needs a few hours to charge. There wasn't enough light left last night after we stopped to charge it back up."

He curses and kicks the basket away from his foot. "Fine. Sit right there and don't move until it's time to go then!" He stabs a finger at the ground under our feet.

We sit on the hard rock and watch him stomp around the sled mumbling to himself until he starts pulling bins, boxes, and bags off of the sled and going through each one. I have to bite my lip hard not to scream at him when he starts throwing our belongings over his shoulder to be discarded. Glo's clutching my arm as he tosses all the little mementos that we have left from our home like garbage. By the time he's done, all that's left besides the boxes of rations and water jugs are the wooden chest with my plant clippings and my two small, stunted potted trees. When he flips the lid open I force myself to look away and bite harder on my lip until blood fills my mouth. There's a chance that we'll be able to escape him at some point and come back to collect all of our things but if I show him how much I value those clippings, he'll rip them to shreds just to torture me.

I hear the thunks of the chest and pots hitting the ground but I'm too afraid to look so when Glo's grip on my arm eases and becomes a rub, I take that as a good sign that he's just discarded them and not destroyed the contents.

"If we're just going to sit here, then make yourself useful and start cooking some food. Make enough for a couple days so I don't have to worry about it on the way back." He barks in my direction, before sitting in a spot of shade with one of the few books I had packed and a shirt full of the tiny oranges and limes that he's stripped from the trees. A snarky reply is on the tip of my tongue about him not being able to read but I swallow it down as Glo and I get up and move to the food to start cooking. It's not lost on me that he said "***his*** way back" and not "***our*** way back." It's just one more confirmation that he plans on either killing us when we get to the claim or just tying us up and leaving us there to die.

When Boyd discarded our belongings, he tossed all the cooking gear as well so I have to sort through the mess to find everything I need. Glo takes that opportunity to scoop soil back into the tree pots and stand them back up. She nudges both the pots and the chest closer to the rock wall so they will be in shade for part of the day. I give her a grateful smile for that and she silently tilts her head towards the water jugs on the sled. I sneak a glance at Boyd but he's busy peeling our fruit so I give her a small nod. She slides closer to the sled and snags one of the partially empty jugs while I gather the pans and small stove to give her cover. I try and keep my head on a swivel like I'm searching for things I need to cook as I watch Boyd to make sure he doesn't look over and see her watering the pots and dumping the rest of the water into the chest. When she slides back over to me and takes a pot and pan from the pile in my arms, I let out the breath I've been holding. It's not much of a victory but at least the plants will live for a few more days unattended if we can get out of this mess.

We set up a cooking area and go rescue the basket from where Boyd had kicked it. Being tied together makes these chores slightly more difficult but I feel better with her by my side instead of being Boyd's body hostage. I don't know if he'll allow us to eat anything later in the day so as I cook the food we nibble away at it. I spend the next hour making easy to eat food, wrapping it up in cloth and packing it away in the basket for later. I make little pouches of nuts and dried fruit and make Glo fill her pockets with them so if the worst happens we'll have something to eat we can sneak later. I fill my own pockets with tightly rolled tortilla spread with protein past and seasoning. Most likely, they'll be a mushy mess by the end of the day but we'll eat them anyway if we have too.

I've just closed up the basket and am getting ready to clean up the cooking gear when a shadow falls over me.

"Leave it and let's go. That thing has charged enough for now." Boyd commands with a painful nudge of his boot in my ribs.

I scoot away from him and help Glo to her feet as he scoops up the basket and drops it on the sled. We fold all the panels back into the sled and latch the bumpers into place and then start it up. It raises up off of the ground and I'm about to send it forwards when Boyd steps up onto it and sits right in the middle of it. He gives me a satisfied grin.

"Lost a lot of dead weight so it shouldn't have a problem carrying me now, right?"

I don't give him the satisfaction of a reply just turn and start the sled moving. My biggest challenge will be not rolling around laughing when he slides right off of the sled when we go down the steep hill ahead. It only takes a few minutes for us to get the ledge and seconds after we go over before he's letting out a strangled, "Whoa! Stop! Stop this thing!"

He slides to the front and climbs over barrier guard that's holding all the bins back when I bring it to a stop and sends me a glare before waving me, the sled, and Glo on ahead. I swear I kept my expression blank but he must have seen something in my eyes because when I pass him, he reaches out and slaps the back of my head leaving my scalp stinging and my eyes watering.

There are only a few really steep spots that we have to manage with most of the path having switchbacks that zig zag down. Climbing up the other side will be brutal. Judging by the sun, I estimate we'll make the top of the climb by noon. I hope Boyd will let us rest there for a bit as we'll be wiped out as we reach the hottest part of the day.

When we get to the bottom, he has me stop the sled again and climbs back onto it. He settles with his back to the path ahead and his feet braced on the rear barrier to prevent himself from sliding off as the sled tilts for the angle of the hill. This time I let my disgust of him show briefly before dropping my head and starting the climb. I keep one hand on Glo to help her and one hand on the remote in case I get the chance to flip it or smash it or…blow it up if I could!

We've barely made it half way up when Glo starts stumbling and I have to practically drag her along with me. I ask Boyd for water for her but he just points to the top. I pull her along with me but after ten minutes, she goes down for good. I ignore Boyd's yells when I bring the sled to a stop, turn and lift Glo up and set her on the sled.

"You tied us together! I can't go any faster than she can. Please, Boyd, let her ride the rest of the way up so we can get this climb done!"

He opens his mouth to yell but then slams it shut and stabs a finger ahead so I get the sled moving again. I thought I could go faster with Glo off her feet but it's just as hard because I'm forced to walk beside the sled with the rope tethering us. I just put my head down and let the rage build as I imagine all the pain and torture I'd like to inflict on him. The rage takes me most of the way to the top but by the time we crest the hill, I just want him to die. I no longer care about all the ways to make him pay, I just want this over.

I stop the sled on level ground and drop to my knees beside it to catch my breath. The sun is so hot and it feels like it's frying the sweat I've built up from the climb right through my clothes. I just want to sit and drink water for a few minutes but Boyd steps off the sled and drops Glo to the ground beside me.

"Let's go. That took way too long. I want to get to the gold today."

I use the sled to pull myself back to my feet and pull Glo up as well as he strides ahead. As we start following him, I snatch a jug of water and take deep swallows until my stomach hurts. I no longer care about rationing it. I'm not going to be able to keep going without it. I pass it back to Glo and hear her gulping it as well. As we trudge after Boyd, I start thinking about my grandfather and water. There's no way he could carry in enough water to stay on his claim for weeks at a time so he must either have a water source or storage at his claims. I pray that's true if we can't get away from Boyd and he leaves us there to die.

Thankfully, the way ahead is more manageable with no more crazy ups and downs. We trudge along slowly in the hot sun and even Boyd is forced to slow right down in the heat. He stays ahead of us for most of the afternoon but looks back frequently to make sure we haven't made a run for it. I'm not sure where we would even run to at this point. A couple of times I position Glo ahead of me to block Boyd's view in case he looks back, and check the map. There's only one more main feature between us and the claim and from the map, it looks like some kind of bridge. I marvel at the things my grandfather was able to accomplish in his day. He had access to advanced technology and unlimited supplies it seems, but it still would have taken a huge amount of work to construct the camouflaged cavern and build bridges out here all alone. He must have been an amazing man and I wish I could have known him. How different our lives might have been if he hadn't died so young.

"He's stopping," Glo whispers to me, breaking me out of my thoughts.

I look up from the ground I'd been focusing on for so long and am surprised that the sun is getting lower in the sky behind me and shadows are starting to fill the landscape. I also become aware of the sluggish hum from the sled. Without a full charge this morning and the strain of carrying Boyd up the hill, the battery is almost done. Maybe I should have been charging as we went the last few hours but I'm glad I didn't think of it because now we can stop and rest for the night.

We catch up to Boyd and he's standing before the mouth of a bridge that spans a twenty-foot divide in the landscape. Unlike the planks from the last small gap, this bridge has waist high pillars with thick chains anchoring it to the rock. The cross boards are the same type of plastic wood from before but this time they are threaded through with more chain.

Boyd unties me from Glo and gives me a shove towards the bridge.

"You first! If that thing is rotted through, you'll know soon enough."

I let out a deeply weary sigh and take a step but before I get to the bridge, a low beeping noise rings out. Boyd goes nuts, pulling out his gun and pointing it in all directions.

"What the hell is that? What's that noise? Where's it coming from?" His voice is frantic like any minute now we're going to come under attack. Glo's tiny squeak of a voice has him freezing in place.

"It's the low battery warning from the sled."

If I had any energy left, I'd laugh right out loud at the look on his face as it flushes red. Thankfully, I don't or he'd probably beat me half to death from his embarrassment at overreacting to something so silly.

He looks between Glo and me as we stand, staring at him and wait for instructions. It seems to make him even angrier. I swear steam comes out of his ears when he screams at me.

"Get that thing opened up and charging. We camp here tonight!"

He shoves past me and starts hauling on the pillars to see if they are firmly stuck in the ground so I send Glo an exaggerated eye roll and get the first smile from her in two days. We're old pros at opening up the solar panels by now so it only takes us a few minutes. I snag the basket from the sled while Boyd's back is still turned and pull out two of the wraps, hand one to Glo and nod to a rock a few feet away where we quickly sit and start eating.

When he's satisfied with the stability of the bridge supports he comes back towards us but pauses when he sees us eating. He doesn't say anything but his mouth goes flat, hard, and mean before he snags the basket and gets his own food. The three of us sit in silence eating our meal but Boyd's eyes never leave us and they're full of malice.

As soon as he swallows the last bite of food, he stands up and comes over to us. When he grabs Glo's arm and hauls her away, she digs in her heels but she's no match for his brute strength. I want to fly at him and scratch his eyes out but I know it will have no effect on him so when he starts looping rope around her, I sit tight figuring he's going to tie us up like he did last night. He's using more rope than he did before though. There's a loop around her thighs, one around her butt and a final one under her arms. I don't really get the point of tying her up that way but I don't really understand most things about Boyd.

I shoot to my feet in concern when he shoves her over to the bridge but he just loops a few coils around the pillar like she's a dog on a leash. Once he's knotted it, he pulls her away from the pillar a few steps and turns to me.

"I think it's time we had that…talk."

As soon as he sees the fear fill my eyes he grins and shoves Glo out and over the edge of the chasm. Her scream of terror as she drops out of sight mixes with the one that rips from my chest until they echo on the rock all around us, sounding like a roar.

Chapter Thirty-Two

Pain is my constant companion. It has stayed with me every step of the hike and not long after the sun came up, its friend burn joined us. The pack on my back is my tormentor. Its weight keeps me bowed but also pushes me forward. I haven't stopped since I left the cavern, afraid that I won't be able to start again. I just keep my eyes on the path ahead of me, watching for their footprints in the dust, move one foot forward and repeat. The sun shining directly down on me tells me it's noon or close to it, but time doesn't matter anymore, only the next step.

The bag on the ground comes into my field of vision but before I can process it, my feet have stumbled over it sending me crashing down to the rock. All I can do is lay there for a few minutes and blink away the stars that swim in my vision. The weight of the pack keeps me pinned to the ground when I finally get the energy to try and stand so I just roll to the side and unclip the straps and slide my arms out. Free of the weight for the first time in close to seven hours, I feel light as a feather.

I push myself up onto my knees and look around the area, confused at what I'm seeing. There's stuff everywhere. Clothes are strewn on the ground between boxes and bags. There's a stove with a dirty pan on it not far away but it's the green over by a rock wall that catches my interest the most. I push to my feet and stagger over to it. Claudia's two small fruit trees rest in the shade. I don't understand this at all. Why would they leave all of their stuff here? I can't see her throwing all of her and Glo's stuff around like this but I can see my brother doing it. A cold finger of terror shoots down my spine as I whirl around and search the whole area for their bodies. My heart only stops racing when I can't find them or any sign of violence.

I walk ahead on the path and take a look down into a steep valley and sigh. That's going to be a brutal descent and then climb to get through with the pack. I'm about to turn and retrieve it to get going again when a flash from the other side of the valley pulls my eyes back. I squint and try to make out what caused the flash but it's too far away to make out anything but bumps and mounds in the landscape. I strain my eyes but nothing really comes clear until I register that a few of the bumps that were there have disappeared. I close my eyes and think hard. Is it them? Could it have been their outlines that disappeared? Could I really have caught up to them?

I turn away from the view and march back to my pack. Glo would have slowed them down. Her short little legs wouldn't have been able to go as fast as Día and Boyd, so he would have been forced to go at her pace. The sled would also take time to recharge so it's possible that I have made up some of the time on them. I drop to my knees and open the pack and take a page from my brother's book. I start lightening my load. Everything comes out and I look it all over before shaking my head. No, no pack at all, just the water, a knife, a flashlight and the gun. That's all I'm going to take. I spend fifteen minutes resting while I eat another of the MRE's, chew down the last six pills and drink as much from the built-in water canteen as I can. I cram the rest of what I'm taking into my pockets, grab the spare container of water and leave. Hopefully, if everything goes well, the three of us will be coming back here soon and can retrieve all of the things we've left.

Going down the hill without the pack on my back feels amazing and by the time I hit the bottom and start up the other side the pain has backed off again. Sadly, it only lasts until I'm halfway up the other side. The steep incline is punishing and I often end up dropping to my knees and crawling up some of it. I'm forced to take many breaks as darkness starts to crowd my vision again. No amount of food or old pills can make up for the injuries and stress I've put on my body.

When I crawl over the edge to level ground I lay there and float away for a while. A parched throat finally has me rolling over, sitting up and fumbling the water container to my lips. All I want to do is lie back down. I don't even care about the pounding sun. I just want to lay here and sleep until I recover. Thoughts of Boyd discarding my friends like he did their belongings flood through my tired brain and that's all I need to reach down deep to find the will to climb to my feet. Those two girls are all I have left in this world. They're my family and I'm not going to let the man that calls himself brother take them away like he has everything else. Not stopping and resting now might kill me but it will be worth it if I can catch up to the girls and end my brother. At least I know I'll die doing the right thing. I have a lot to make up for after years of going along with Boyd's will.

I take one last drink of water, cap the container and start moving again. I drop my head and focus on the ground at my feet, find a decent rhythm and zone out. I know time is passing by the burn of the sun as it drops down my back but I just keep going in a zoned-out daze until I hear something different causing my head to snap up.

"I think it's time we had that…talk."

My eyes focus on my brother not more than twenty feet away. A split second later, my eyes drop and meet Glo's who is standing beside him. Her eyes flare wide when she sees me just as she goes flying backward and drops from sight.

I think I hear screaming but my roar of anguish drowns them out. Boyd's got the stupidest grin on his face like pushing little girls off cliffs is all fun and games but it quickly morphs into shock when he sees me. My hand was reaching for the gun as soon as I saw him but froze on the handle when Glo disappeared. I yank it out of my pocket, cock the hammer and point it at him. He has one second to halfway lift his hand like he's asking me to stop before I return the greeting he gave me the day before.

"Goodbye, brother."

I pull the trigger. The shot echoes against the rock as he flies backward just like Glo did and disappears from view. The gun drops from my numb hand and my head turns to Día when she yells out Glo's and then my name. I didn't even see her there. I thought Boyd had pushed her over the cliff too. At least I got here in time to save her but I doubt she'll forgive me now that Glo's gone. I take one step towards her to tell her how sorry I am that I failed her but the adrenaline that has been keeping me on my feet has left and the ground rushes up to meet me.

Chapter Thirty-Three

Gloria! Beck, Boyd! What just happened? I feel like I'm going to puke as I try and process WHAT JUST HAPPENED. I stagger towards Beck who has fallen flat on his face but change directions when I hear Glo scream my name. What the hell! He pushed her. He pushed her off the edge! How could he do that? How could anyone do such a thing to a child? I'm gasping for breath as sobs rack my chest when I drop to my knees at the edge and cling to the pillar so I can look over it. I can't see the bottom it's so deep and dark with the sun almost set. I can't see Glo either but I can hear her sobbing my name and the rope under my hand on the pillar is twisting. She's there, she's down there! He tied her up before he pushed her!

I grab the rope and start hauling on it but it's so heavy and it keeps twisting in my hands.

"Glo! Glo, I need you to listen to me!" I keep yelling until she finally answers back.

"Honey, I need your help to get you back up! You need to stop twisting. Can you feel the wall? I need you to put your feet on the wall and walk up as I pull on the rope! Can you do that? Can you help me?"

Silence greets me and I think I've lost her. I'm about to yell again when the rope twists a last time and then goes steady and her small, scared voice floats up to me.

"I'm ready, start pulling."

I don't waste my breath on any more yelling, just start hauling on the rope. One agonizing foot at a time it comes up until I finally see her head come into view and her tiny hands clutch at the edge. I keep hold of the rope with one hand and grab her wrist to pull her the rest of the way over. We collapse in each other's arms sobbing and clutching at each other.

I almost lost her. I almost lost the most important thing in my world. If not for…Beck! I set Glo aside, push to my feet and rush over to him. He's face first on the ground and my hands hover over him afraid of what I will find when I turn him over. I finally swallow down the fear and gently roll him over. Again, I hesitate, but I need to know - so I press two fingers to his neck and wait. A shudder goes through me when at first I feel nothing. I drop my head as a wash of sorrow steals over me but seconds later, I feel it. It's faint but it's there, he's alive! Glo drops down beside me as I look him over. He's wearing a different set of clothes than the last time I saw him and there's a piece of shiny silver tape on his forehead. I know Boyd shot him, I saw the pool of blood he was in as we left him so I gently lift his shirt. I find more of the silver tape wrapped around his waist with a bump where I'm guessing a bandage is under it. I don't see any bleeding and I have no supplies to treat him with so I just lower the shirt and lean back.

"Is Beck going to be ok? Did he push Boyd off the edge?"

I wrap my arm around my little sister just to feel her near me. "I don't know. I hope so. He shot Boyd and that made him fall off the edge."

"So, Boyd's gone? Like forever … dead?"

I rest my head on hers and just breathe in the smell of Glo. "Yes. If the bullet didn't kill him then the fall did. He's gone, forever, and he won't be able to hurt us again."

Glo sighs, "That's good. He was really mean!"

I let out a choked laugh at that understatement and we just sit there in the fading light of a horrific day. There's nothing I can do now until the sun comes up so we eventually lay down next to Beck and go to sleep. I can only hope he makes it through the night.

When we wake, the sun's been up for a few hours. After the last two exhausting days, our bodies needed the extra rest. Beck is still alive but he's also still out cold. I dribble some water into his mouth and see him swallow so I take that as a good sign and hope his body is just in healing mode. Glo and I eat a quick breakfast when we see that the sled is back to a full charge and bring it over to where Beck lies. I need to get him on the sled but I'm afraid moving him will hurt him. There's nothing I can do about that so I just go for it. A little bit of pain is better than leaving him out here in the sun. I grip him under his arms and drag him up and onto the sled with a little bit of help from Glo. We pile the supplies around him and position the umbrellas over him so he'll be shaded from the sun.

Once we're ready, I look at the bridge and past it towards my grandfather's claim and then turn away. I don't care about gold. I care about life. We retrace our footsteps from yesterday and at the steep hill, Glo gets on the sled and holds Beck in place so he won't slide off. I don't know why but it feels more manageable this time. Maybe it's because we're headed toward the valley and life, instead of a dead gold claim with a dead man. Maybe it's the freedom from Boyd that makes it feel easier. We reach the top of the other side as the sun sinks down behind the rocks and I'm pleased to see all of our supplies still scattered around that Boyd had discarded. Glo and I go to work gathering it all back up into a pile beside the sled and she drags over a pack I don't recognize. I can only assume it came from Beck so I empty it out and go through the contents. When I look inside the box with a red cross on it I'm happy with what I find. Beck's wounds will need to be cleaned and the wrappings changed if we want to prevent infection and I now have the supplies to do that.

We set up our meager camp and eat for the night and I decide to wait for the morning to address Beck's wounds when the light will be better. I hope he'll wake up soon. Glo and I have been taking turns all day dribbling water into him but he has to need more than that as well as some food to help him heal.

I wake up to the sound of groaning and jerk to a sitting position causing Glo to flop off of me with a grunt from where she had cuddled up to me in the night. I swing my head around and a grin spreads across my face when my eyes meet Beck's. I crawl over to the sled and reach out to put my hand on his cheek.

"The hero awakens!"

His eyes are filled with confusion for a moment and then turn to pain filled when the memories of what happened flood back.

"Glo, Gloria. I'm so sorry, Día. I tried to get to you in time. I tried…"

He trails off when Glo sits up beside me and gives him a little wave. Beck's mouth drops open as he stares in shock at her and then swings his gaze back to me.

"What? How? I saw her go over! I saw Boyd…"

Glo answers him while I just grin. "He tied me up to the post on the bridge before he pushed me so I didn't go all the way down! Did you know you can walk up a wall? I didn't know that until Día told me I could!"

He chokes out a laugh that turns into a groan. "I'm very happy that you're ok. I thought I had lost you." He swallows painfully then asks, "Can I have some water?"

Glo and I jump into nurse mode, getting him propped up against some boxes and trying to give him water from a jug. He tells us about the built-in water canteen with tubing in his pack so we top it off and leave it beside him so he can sip from it instead of the heavy jug. We make him eat a small meal even though he claims not to want anything and once he is done I set the med kit on the sled beside him and open it.

He eyes it warily. "I think it's fine, Día. We should just leave it to heal."

I give him a patronizing look. "And then it will fester with infection and you're dead. Sorry Beck but that tape is coming off!"

He looks away with a grimace and lifts a hand in a go-ahead motion. I get his shirt off and then lay him back down before going to work on removing the tape that's wrapped all the way around his waist. The skin pulls in a few places but a lot of it is barely hanging on from the motions of his body and sweat since he applied it. When I finally get the last of it off and peel back the bloody and spongy gauze that's stuck to the wound on his front, I see an ugly hole that's red and swollen. It hasn't started to smell yet but it's definitely on its way to being infected. I sit back on my heels and think about what we have in the supplies that Abuela had packed. With all the hospitals and clinics in our town closing years ago, she had been forced to use herbal remedies from plants in our atrium for many of the small injuries and illnesses that Glo and I had growing up. I know she packed a box with her dried herbs that she called her medical kit so I get up and start searching for it.

When I find what I'm looking for, I bring it back to the sled and sort through it for the dried garlic bulbs. Abuela has packed the small ceramic bowl and pestle so I crush the garlic and add drops of water until I have a decent paste. I pull out a small stack of clean rags that she has in the box and after cleaning both the front and back wounds I apply it generously to both areas. I saw a tensor bandage in the med kit from Beck's pack so I unroll it and wrap him back up.

"That stinks!" He complains when I'm done.

I smile while tidying everything back up. "Yes, it does - but it will hopefully stop that infection from taking hold and it should also help with some of the pain."

He grabs my wrist as I start to stand. "Claudia, thank you. Thank you for taking care of me and…for not blaming me for my brother."

When he looks away in shame, I grab his chin and force him to look at me.

"You are NOT responsible for your brother! He made his own choice and he chose to be a horrible person. That's not on you. Besides, you saved us. If you hadn't shown up when you did, well it was about to get really ugly so let it go. He's gone, we're free of him now."

He gives me a small grateful smile and eases back down on the sled so I set the umbrellas back up to shade him and Glo and I work on arranging the rest of our supplies around him so we can get going. He spends most of the day sleeping, as Glo and I hike, only waking for water and a little bit of food. We take it easy and don't push our speed even though I'm starting to worry about how much water we have left. Even though I've committed to the belief that the valley is there waiting for us, I'll still hedge my bets and keep at least two jugs of water in reserve.

By the end of our second day of hiking, Beck's able to walk beside the sled for twenty minutes at a time. His wounds are no longer red and he shows no sign of a fever so I know with time he will heal. I also know that once we get to the valley, I'm going to have to stitch those holes up with the needle and thread he had in the kit. I keep that information to myself for now otherwise he might turn and bolt in the opposite direction!

When we wake on the third morning, I know we are close. There's nothing on the map ahead of us but the valley. All the urgency I felt about getting there has drained away and I find myself stalling once the sled is back to a full charge. It's like I'd rather just keep the idea of the valley instead of taking the chance of being disappointed by the reality of it. Abuela said it's there, the pictures show it's there, even my grandfather's old friend Charlie said it's there, but I just can't help thinking it is too good to be true.

I find myself following behind the others and the sled as my steps are slower today. Glo is skipping out front while Beck walks beside the sled with the remote. My head snaps up and my feet freeze in place when Glo calls out.

"Hey! There's a big hole here we have to cross!"

I want to turn around. I want to just turn around and go back to the cart because I know now. The only hole in front of us on the map would be the valley and if she's not screaming with happiness from all the green foliage and the gushing water then that means it's not there. I watch Beck as he joins her at the edge, my eyes fixed on his back as he just stands there and stares down. When he turns and beckons me forward, it's not with a smile but with a blank expression.

I don't want to go. I don't want to look at it but my feet start moving forward anyway. I reach the edge and look down. I see brown, yellow, and hints of red here and there but I don't see green and I certainly don't see the most important…blue. My eyes follow the dried stream bed up the length of the valley to the rock wall that should have a gushing waterfall and instead see a glimmer of wetness that trickles down the wall to a tiny spec of the green I was so desperate to see. There was water here once but it's long gone now. My eyes drift to where the house should be but even it's gone. There's just a sheet of rock where the picture showed it to be.

I slowly sink down until I'm sitting on the ground and close my eyes so I don't have to look at what isn't there anymore.

Chapter Thirty-Four

"We should go down," Beck says from where he's sat down beside me.

I don't bother to open my eyes when I reply. "No, we should go back. Figure out where to go next."

He doesn't answer me so after a few minutes of silence I open my eyes and look his way but he's just staring intently down into the empty valley.

"What's the point, Beck? There's nothing here for us. There might have been a long time ago but it's all gone now."

He finally turns his head in my direction but instead of answering me he asks a question.

"Can I see the pictures, please?"

I shake my head. "It isn't there, Beck! It doesn't matter what the pictures show. THERE IS NOTHING THERE!"

He just shrugs annoyingly and holds out his hand for the pictures. I huff out a breath of frustration but open my bag and pull them out for him. I turn away from him as he studies them and I look to Glo. She is sitting a few feet away with her matchstick legs crossed and her pointed chin resting on a fist as she looks longingly down into what might have been. I'm about to slide over to her and take her into my arms when Beck lets out a bark of laughter. Both Glo and I snap our heads in his direction and see him push to his feet with a grin on his face.

He looks down at us and says, "Your grandfather was just like the coyote!" When we just stare at him like he's lost his mind, he laughs again. "He's a trickster! Come on, I'm going down there and you should too!"

I don't get a chance to say anything before he powers up the sled and sends it down the path that zig zags down the side of the valley wall and then follows behind it. I turn to Glo who's jumped to her feet and with a shrug and a grin at me, heads after him. I sit there and dig my heels in the ground to make divots and stall like a pouty child. What's the point of wasting energy going down there and then having to climb back up? And what does Beck mean about the whole trickster thing? I kick up more dust and think about the tricks my grandfather has played to keep his mining locations a secret. A hidden hand cart that rides on overlooked, unused tracks. A cavern to hide away the cart with walls that look like rock but aren't rock. Wood that looks like wood but isn't. So is Beck saying that the empty valley isn't empty after all?

I push to my feet and look again but I just don't see what he could have seen to change his mind from up here so I let my shoulders slump and trudge down the path after them. At the very least we might be able to fill some of our jugs from that trickle of water coming out of the end of the valley's wall.

It doesn't take me long to catch up to them and when we reach the floor I mumble under my breath just loud enough for Beck to hear.

"Total waste of time and energy."

He doesn't reply, just nudges me with his shoulder and winks at me with that stupid grin of his. I roll my eyes but keep walking as he heads straight for the sheet of stone where the picture showed a house being there instead. The closer we get, the slower I walk as a flutter starts in my chest while I study the rock ahead. It looks sheer and smooth, nothing like the other rocks in this area. It almost looks like…I stop the thought when Beck grabs my arm and pulls me to a stop when we are only ten feet away from it. He reaches down and picks up a fist sized stone and holds it out to me.

"Throw it."

I look at the rock in his hand and then back to the smooth angled rock mound ahead of us and swallow down the hope that's starting to build in my chest. I shake my head.

"You do it. You throw it." I say in the quietest voice.

He studies my face for a few seconds and then nods. He whips his arm back and lets the rock fly. We all stand there until Glo starts giggling because instead of the hard thwack of rock meeting rock that should have happened when it connected, it made no sound at all. It just bounced right off. She's laughing as she launches herself at the rock and runs right into it. I can see the rock that's not a rock give when her weight hits it but then I can't see anything else as decades of sand and dust come billowing off of it into a giant cloud.

The three of us quickly retreat to halfway down the valley and wait for the dust cloud to settle.

"The house is under there, isn't it?" Glo asks while we wait. I nod my head that yes, I think it's there. "Does that mean the waterfall is hiding too?"

I open my mouth to tell her no, that the water has dried up here like everywhere else but stop and turn to Beck with a raised eyebrow. I've been wrong about everything else so…

He looks down at the wall where the water trickles and cocks his head before answering.

"You know, being a miner means that you need to know a lot about rock. You have to know how to drill into it and shore it up with supports or how to safely blow it up. He found a way to hide the house so no one would find it but the biggest draw to this valley would have been the water so I'm going to bet that he figured out a way to plug it up. I'm going to bet that it's there waiting and we're going to find a way to get it flowing again." He throws an arm around each of our shoulders. "Come on, the dust is settling. Let's go uncover our new home!"

Epilogue

I finish tidying up our dinner dishes and grab the broom to sweep the floor under the kitchen table. There's a pretty rug underneath it but it makes it hard to clean up the crumbs that get on it so I end up just moving the table and pulling up the rug to take it outside and shake out. My hands still as I see the trap door that was hidden by the rug and I gently drop it to the side and get down on my knees. I smile when I think about all the tricks my grandfather has played on us and wonder what this one will be.

I pull the ring and the door comes up easily. There's still enough light for me to clearly see the stacked bars that fill the opening. I stare at it for a few minutes before shaking my head and closing the door. I replace the rug without bothering to shake it off and move the table back into its place.

I'm still shaking my head with a small smile as I go out to the front porch and settle into the double rocker beside Beck. I lean my head on his shoulder and think about everything it took for us to get here. Once again, I have the same thought as before. I don't care about gold bars, I care about life. I sigh with contentment as we sit there watching Glo dance and laugh in the mist that our gushing waterfall kicks up, happy.

Excerpt from a private letter.

April 3, 2031

To my loving wife,

I want to start this letter by apologizing to you. I should never have left for this trip until we had resolved our argument. I hate knowing that we parted with anger in our hearts. I've had plenty of time to think about your reasons for not wanting to relocate to the valley and I want to tell you that I understand. I understand all the reasons you've listed for not wanting to be so isolated with our small daughter. I want only the best for both of you but most of all I only want happiness for you.

This will be my second to last trip into these hills and then my time as a prospector will be over. I have brought in all the materials that I will need to close up and camouflage the valley so that it will be here as a fallback option should the very worst happen. I've spent days hanging in a harness on the side of the valley wall while I drill into the stone to install the sluice gate that will close off the water and hopefully keep it from drying up like so many other sources have. At night, I sew the tarps together by lantern light so that I can cover the house. Hopefully, these measures will be enough to stop anyone who stumbles on the valley from entering it and discovering the preparations I've made for us.

I concede to you that we will not move to the valley but the writing is on the wall as far as us losing the war and that means we will not be able to stay in California. I refuse to return north and live under the government that took over my home country and annex it to be a new nation with the northern states. Instead, we will go south! Yes, I said south. Far south down to the tip of South America. With the temperatures rising everywhere and the U.S gone from most trade pacts, the countries down there are flourishing in both economics and environments. The government of Argentina was most eager to grant us citizenship with passports when I moved the majority of our fortune to their main bank. I have stockpiled a large sum of gold bars as well as the passports we will need here in the valley and will come to retrieve them when it's time for us to go. I do not trust the local government not to search and confiscate goods and property once they finally concede that they have lost the war.

My sweet wife, as much as you wish to stay in our home, it just won't be possible if we want our daughter to be safe. I must insist that you concede to my wishes just as I have conceded to yours in regards to the valley. Please, sweetheart, give some deep thought until I'm back and we will discuss it in more detail once I'm home.

All my love to you and our daughter,

Lucas

Coming Soon….

Sun & Smoke, Book Three in the Endless Winter series.

Read on for an excerpt from Land – A Stranded Novel, book one in the Stranded series available at all retailers FREE.

Sign up to my newsletter to be notified of new releases and special discounted prices.

Please visit: http://www.theresashaver.com/

Excerpt: Land - Chapter 1

Alex looked around at the bright, overly decorated buildings on Main St. Disneyland and gave a sigh as she pushed a golden red curl out of her green eyes.

"This would have been a lot more fun if we could have been here when we were ten." she said, turning to her best friend Emily.

Emily was busy scrolling through her iPhone and didn't even hear her. Alex was glad that they were going to have a chance to spend some time together. It seemed to her that they had hardly spoken in the last three months since Emily had started dating Mason. Growing up together on neighbouring farms in Alberta, they had been inseparable since they got on the same school bus for their first day of kindergarten. They had grown up with all the same interests and hobbies until age thirteen when Alex started to get serious about gymnastics and Emily decided swimming was her favourite. Even different sporting schedules had not deterred them from BFF status. But now at sixteen, it seemed there was finally a huge obstacle in the way of their friendship.

Alex looked over at Mason and his group of friends standing apart from the rest of the class. As always, Mason was holding court and Lisa, the "prom queen" wannabe along with Mark, the "bully sidekick" were hanging on to the football quarterback's every word. Alex could understand Emily's attraction to the guy. He was tall and broad with sun-streaked brown hair that fell over his forehead in a dreamy kind of way. His eyes matched his hair, a golden brown hazel surrounded by eyelashes any girl would kill for. So yeah, standing here looking at Mason, any girl would get a flutter as long as you just looked. Within minutes of talking to the guy though, that flutter should turn to stone. Mason was one of those jocks that was all about himself and needed constant adoration. Once again, it baffled Alex as to why her best friend was dating the jerk. Both girls were on the honour roll and volunteered for extra credit. Emily having way more patience had started tutoring and that's how the Mason thing started. After a week of tutoring Mason, Emily had started walking the halls, holding hands with him and sitting with his group at lunch. When Alex had tried talking to her about it, she had brushed Alex off, saying that she was too judgmental and if she really knew Mason she would like him too.

After that Emily drifted further away and rarely did anything with Alex. "I really miss her but she has changed so much." thought Alex.

Looking around at the rest of her class she saw some of her other friends in a group and realized that the class was divided mainly into two groups – farm and town. With another sigh, Alex thought about how Emily wasn't really in the farm group anymore.

Mr. Carter was trying to get the class to move closer together so he could give out the schedule for the day and wasn't having much luck. The kids were excited and distracted by being in Disneyland. It still amazed Alex that somehow her class won this trip by having the highest test scores in the whole province. Bringing more than twenty teenagers to California seemed a little crazy to Alex even with three teachers and two parent chaperones. When she first found out about the trip, Alex didn't really want to go. She figured it would be a bit of a gong show with some of the town kids getting out of control and she felt Disneyland was made for a much younger crowd. Surprisingly it was Emily who convinced her to come, saying it would give them a chance to reconnect and spend time together.

Emily had said that she would really like to room together in the hotel. Alex was really happy to hear this because she had heard Lisa telling another girl that she and Em were going to room together and Alex had been jealous not to be rooming with her friend.

Last night in the hotel, Alex and Emily stayed up late and talked about a lot of things that had happened in the last few months. They felt reconnected after not spending time together. Alex talked about her gymnastics and other things in her life and Emily confessed her confusion over Mason.

"I don't think I'm ready for what he wants. He suggested that this trip would be a good time for us to "take the next step" but we've only been dating for a few months and I'm not sure I want to go there yet." Emily said with a frown.

Alex was used to her friend being more assertive and sure of herself so she tried to help.

"Just tell him how you feel and make it clear so there's no confusion." she advised.

Emily grimaced, "You don't know Mason. He doesn't like to be told no. I'm just so glad you decided to room with me. I overheard him telling Lisa that he'd let her know what night he wanted her out of the room. I didn't want to let that happen so thanks again for staying with me." she smiled gratefully at Alex.

Alex was shocked. That's why Emily wanted her here, to run interference? After the disappointment and loneliness of the past few months without her friend, Alex was mad and blasted her friend.

"Really Em?! That's why you convinced me to come, so I could protect you from your bully of a boyfriend? Really? How stupid am I that I thought you missed me and wanted to spend time with me? Unbelievable! Well if that's all you need me for, then forget it! You're my best friend but three months ago you dumped me for a guy. A guy who you can't even say no to, you can't treat me like that and then expect me to just snap to it when you need help!" she turned away with frustrated tears in her eyes.

Alex stared at the hotel's bland wallpaper waiting for a response from Emily. When none came she whirled around ready to yell and saw her friend staring down into her lap with tears flowing down her face. All the anger left Alex and she slumped down beside her and put her arm around her shoulder. They sat like that for a while until Emily composed herself and started to quietly talk.

"You're right Alex. I owe you an apology. I have put Mason ahead of you and I'm so sorry. He really isn't a bully. He's just strong willed. I really like him. He's so different when it's just the two of us together. I know if you got to know him you'd see a different side of him. Please, Alex, forgive me? I didn't just ask you to room with me to put him off. I really miss you and wanted time with you too. Please understand."

Alex sighed in frustration, "I can't get to know him if we never hang out Em. I miss you, we all miss you. I promise to make the effort to get to know him better if we start spending time together again. I love you and just want my BFF back, Ok?"

Emily brushed her tears away and threw her arms around her best friend. They spent the rest of the night gossiping and giggling.

Alex smiled at the memory and looked around at her classmates. She found herself meeting the dark blue eyes that belonged to Cooper Morris. The amused mocking smirk on his face made Alex quickly look away. She didn't know why Cooper always made her feel nervous but found herself often looking in his direction at school and it seemed that most times he was looking right back. Cooper had the bad boy rep at school, dressing the part with a beat up leather jacket, his black hair, dark blue eyes and a devilish grin. It seemed to Alex that it was mainly rumours, but it wasn't like they hung out with the same people so she didn't have a lot of firsthand knowledge about him. After Emily's comment about Alex being judgmental, she was going to try harder to have an open mind about people.

She kept looking around to see if they were going to be allowed to head deeper into Disney when she noticed Quinn and Josh heading in their direction. The boys were good childhood friends of Alex and Emily and had spent a lot of time while growing up together camping and hanging out at the lake, working on 4H projects. The third boy that usually completed their group was David but Alex didn't see him nearby. She wasn't really surprised, as David had been in love with a clueless Emily for forever and he tended to avoid her since she started dating Mason. The boys had also felt Emily's absence in the past few months and were happy to see her and Alex had made up.

"Hey guys! Any idea where you want to go first?" asked Quinn

"I'm hitting Space Mountain until I feel like puking and then I plan on finding Goofy and hurling all over him!" Josh exclaimed.

Alex groaned but had to laugh as it was so typical of Josh and his rough and crazy personality to make such a statement. Quinn punched his friend in the arm and joked, "If you change that to Mickey Mouse, then I could get on board with that plan."

Josh was of medium height and stocky, with a barrel chest and thick muscular arms that he had developed from the hard work he put in on his family's farm. He had curly brown hair and brown eyes that always seemed happy. Quinn had the height and build of a football quarterback, tall and broad with his own muscles. His hair was wavy blond and he had calm blue eyes.

Alex was watching her teacher impatiently, "Looks like Mr. Carter isn't having much luck moving the class together and he's going to each group and giving the schedule out." Alex pointed out.

"Finally! I'm ready to rock this playland." Josh said.

For the first time, Emily looked up from her iPhone and joined the conversation, brushing her long blond hair back impatiently.

"Hey guys, I've been reading the headlines online and something weird seems to be going on." With a worried expression, she explained, "The US government has gone to DEFCON 2 and the news is saying that that means nuclear war is the next step. CNN is saying the last time they went to that level was during the cold war."

"No way man! That would be just our luck. We're like 1500 miles from home and in one of the guaranteed cities that would take a hit!" Josh joked.

"I don't think this is a joke," Emily said seriously. "I think we should tell Mr. Carter about this. I'm really worried."

All the kids in Alex's group turned to look for their teacher and saw him coming towards them. A few steps away and the man seemed to stagger and freeze with wide eyes. Then he swayed and finally toppled to the ground.

To Alex, it seemed as though all sound was sucked out of the world in an instant. Then kids were screaming and yelling and racing towards their teacher. Quinn got to him first and Josh was yelling at Emily to call 911. Alex felt like her feet were glued to the ground. She was looking around Main Street Disney to see if she could spot any security or employees when the realization came to her that this situation was way bigger than her fallen teacher. She could hear plenty of excited voices but nothing else. The music was gone. The sounds of rides, cars, phones ringing, all mechanical sounds were gone, even the huge water fountain in the middle of the square had stopped gushing, the water slowly draining away. At that moment, movement in the air caught her attention and she looked up unbelievingly. A huge airplane was slowly falling out of the sky. It looked like it would hit the ground a few miles away. Alex clutched Emily's arm and pointed up at the plane, still unable to speak. Emily looked up from her dark phone and her mouth dropped open with a whimper.

At this point, Quinn was doing CPR on Mr. Carter and looked over at Emily to see if she was calling 911. As he was about to yell at her, his gaze went up to see what the girls were looking at in terror. When the plane registered in his mind he fell back on his butt and cried out, "NO!"

It seemed that everyone around them was now watching the falling plane. It took what felt like forever for it to finally pass below the horizon but seconds later the explosion was easy to see and hear. Emily turned away and buried her tear-streaked face against Alex's shoulder. Alex was numb with disbelief. "We're at Disneyland. This doesn't happen at Disneyland!" she thought. She gently pushed Emily back and took her phone out of her hand. It was off so she tried to turn it on but nothing was working. She looked around to see if anyone else had a phone and could see lots of other students staring at cell phones that didn't seem to be working.

Someone close by was screaming and it felt like a drill in Alex's ears so she tried to find the source and wasn't that surprised to see the youngest teacher, Ms. Scott belting it out while pulling her hair on both sides of her head. Just as Alex thought she should go get her calmed down, Mrs. Moore, who was the oldest of the teachers and quite the battle axe, grabbed the younger teacher by the shoulders and gave her a quick shake with a stern "Settle down!" When that didn't work she just gave the young teacher a slap across the face. Instant silence from the screaming was the result and Mrs. Moore shoved the shocked teacher at one of the parent chaperones and told her to get her settled down.

With her hands raised in the air, she loudly ordered, "All Prairie Springs students form up on the grass and sit down...NOW!" the last word said with a louder snap. As Mrs. Moore saw students moving onto the grassy area by the street she turned and looked to Alex's group. Quinn was still sitting on the ground beside Mr. Carter and Emily had knelt down on the other side of him and was holding his limp hand. Alex and Josh were standing staring down at him not sure what to do.

Mrs. Moore moved over to them and took a deep breath. "Quinn?"

He looked up at her with a stunned expression on his face and tears shining in his eyes and said, "I think he's dead."

Mrs. Moore leaned over and placed a comforting hand on his shoulder and said in a calm voice "Yes. There was nothing you could have done for him, Quinn. He had a pacemaker and it would have stopped as well. But thank you for trying. You are a good boy."

"I don't understand. What do you mean it would have stopped?" Quinn asked confusion on his face.

"Yes, well. Please join your classmates on the grass and I will try to explain what I think is happening." Mrs. Moore offered.

As Quinn got up off the ground and Alex helped Emily up, Josh was shrugging out of his sweatshirt and went to cover Mr. Carter with it. "Josh, don't do that!" Mrs. Moore barked. At Josh's expression, Mrs. Moore softened and said in a kinder tone, "That is very respectful of you but we must be practical. You will need your sweater later." With a confused look on his face, Josh stepped back and put his sweater back on. Mrs. Moore leaned down and pulled Mr. Carter's jacket up over his face. She then took his money belt off and retrieved his wallet from his pant pocket. She dropped both items into her purse and ushered the group over to the subdued students sitting on the grass. Once they were seated, she took in the whole group and lowered herself to one knee.

"A terrible event has happened and there is no way for me to know the exact details but from what we have seen I can guess what has happened. It appears all electronics are not working and as we saw with the plane falling and crashing many mechanics have also failed. That could only be caused by an EMP. That means an electromagnetic pulse. This happens when a nuclear device is detonated or a massive solar flare from the sun hits earth."

The uproar that followed was full of confused shouts, yelled denials, loud sobbing and wailing. Mrs. Moore raised her hands and waited for the crowd to calm down and was about to speak when Emily stood and turned to the group and loudly stated "I was watching the news on my phone before it went out!" as everyone was now focused on Emily she lowered her voice and told what she had seen on CNN then quickly turned around and sat back down.

"Well, that certainly makes things somewhat clearer. Thank you, Emily, for that information. So we have some important decisions to make and we must make them fairly quickly." Mrs. Moore scanned the group to see if they were following her words and then continued.

"Everything will be different now. We cannot count on the government to take care of us. We will have to take care of ourselves and that means working together. We won't be able to fly home now so we have to decide if or how we will get back to Canada."

Suddenly Mrs. Davis, a parent chaperone, jumped to her feet and said "What are you talking about? Of course we will go home! The authorities will get this straightened out and get us home. We must be patient and wait for help. All this talk of not counting on the government is irresponsible of you. It will only panic the children. I suggest we return to the hotel and wait for the management to sort this out!" she finished while looking around the group for support. Everyone stared at her and then swung their eyes back to Mrs. Moore to see what she would say.

Calmly Mrs. Moore tried to explain the situation. "Mrs. Davis, I understand your reasoning but this is not a normal situation. We can walk back to the hotel but please understand. There will be no power to the elevators so that means climbing 10 flights of stairs as that is the floor we are on. Also, the room doors all have electronic locks that won't be working so we will have to break the doors open. It will also be very dark in the hallways with the lights out. Next, the management and staff are just people like us that will most likely all leave to check on their own families. With almost all transportation not working, the government will not be able to move around to help most people. Therefore as I said, we must take care of ourselves. This will be a huge challenge. Food and water and safety must be our first priority. With no electricity, the water will not flow. With no transportation, food will not be delivered. And finally with over ten million people in this area and no real law enforcement, within days this city will explode with violence. We know of one plane crash but there were probably more which means fires. With the roads blocked by broken down cars and fire trucks not working anyways, the fires will burn out of control. Does everyone understand what I'm saying? The best thing we could do is try to leave this city as soon as possible." and with that final statement Mrs. Moore sat down.

Excerpt: Land - Chapter 2

Alex looked at her watch and was surprised to see that only 20 minutes had passed since all this started. It was only 8:30 am and it felt like late afternoon to her.

"Does your watch work?" came from over her shoulder. She turned and saw it was Quinn asking.

"Yes it's only 8:30." she told him.

"Why do you think your watch works? Mine is dead. It was a digital I got last year." he asked.

"Don't know but maybe because it's really old. I have to wind it every morning. It was my grandmother's."

"Good to know. Some really old stuff might still work," he replied with a smile.

"Listen, if this is what Mrs. Moore is talking about and after what Em saw on CNN it sounds like it is, we really need to come up with a plan and I don't think we should take too long." Quinn advised.

Staring into Quinn's eyes, Alex couldn't help but wonder how he seemed so calm. Living on a farm meant you learned to keep your head in the game and make quick decisions. Working with animals is always tricky and can be unpredictable. But this was so far from anything they could relate to that Alex felt like she was barely holding on. The one thing she did know was that she trusted Quinn a hundred percent. They had been friends forever and he'd always had a good head on his shoulders. Even when Josh was doing crazy stunts or pranks, Quinn could always steer the situation the right way so everything worked out. Alex always thought that sometime in the future she and Quinn would end up together as a couple. It just never seemed to be the right time and they were always so comfortable together that there was never any pressure to be more than the good friends they were.

A sudden thought jumped center stage into Alex's mind. "Oh my God! What about radiation. Don't we have to think about radiation if a nuclear bomb went off!" she gasped.

"Whoa, Ok, hold on. Other than that plane crashing no one saw an explosion or heard anything. No mushroom cloud on the horizon like you always see in the movies, so whatever happened, it wasn't that close but yeah definitely something to keep in mind." he consoled.

"Right now we are in the middle of millions of people and that is really far from my comfort zone. So the sooner we get out of here and into the countryside, the better I'll feel. Let's grab the rest of the gang and talk to Mrs. Moore. No one else seems to be getting it together so let's talk to her and see if she has a plan."

Alex went over to get Emily who was talking to Mason and his friends. When she told Emily what she and Quinn had discussed, Mason jumped in and said they would come talk to Mrs. Moore as well. With a shrug, Alex turned away and headed back to Quinn who had rounded up Josh and found David as well. As her group of students approached Mrs. Moore, Alex noticed others heading the same way. Cooper and Dara, a girl from town with black hair with bright blue streaks running through it, joined up with Quinn's group. Alex arrived in time to hear Quinn ask Mrs. Moore how she knew so much about nuclear bombs.

"Well Dear, I'm a Prepper and have been for years. If you don't know what that is I will explain. There are a lot of people who believe that the world as we know it will someday change drastically. Whether it is a pandemic of some sort, an economical crash or nuclear war, civilization as we know it will end and chaos will ensue. So we prep for it. Knowledge is a Prepper's biggest asset so we research different scenarios and plan for as much as we can so that we will hopefully survive. I must say that for all the prepping I have done over the years, being at Disneyland was not one of the options I was prepared for." Mrs. Moore seemed to be reflecting on that statement and was clearly not pleased. She seemed to center herself and focused back on the group of students surrounding her.

"Alright students, time to make a plan. The best chance of survival is to get away from large populations and that means cities. So as I'm sure no cars are working that means walking. Now it might seem impossible to walk all the way back to Canada but it isn't and people have walked even further. That, of course, is the worst-case scenario. Next would be bikes. Students such as you should easily be able to bike a hundred kilometres a day but probably quite a bit more than that. The best case would be if you could find an older vehicle. Anything in the 70's and older should work just fine. The problem with newer vehicles is that they rely on electronics so they would have shorted out. Older cars don't have many electronics in them so that is good. The bad news is we have to find them."

As she paused to catch her breath Mason jumped in with a question. "So you really don't think there would be any government coming to help?"

Surprisingly it was Dara who offered an opinion. "I like to read apocalyptic books and in every one it's always the people who got out of the cities fast or are already in rural areas that survive. The people who stay in cities, almost always die," she finished.

With a sneer on his face, Mason's friend Mark who was best known as a bully said, "Shut up Freak. No one cares about your dumb Goth punk books."

Dara shook her head with disgust and took a step back. Emily was looking at Mason to say something to his friend but he had a small smirk of his own. Lisa gave a quick giggle but sucked it back when Mrs. Moore glared at her. Quinn took a step toward Mark with an angry face just as Alex loudly called out, "You ass!"

Mrs. Moore took a quick step, blocking Quinn and declared, "Yes. Yes, he is an ass." This made everybody stop and stare at her in shock. No one could believe that a teacher had said such a thing.

"My goodness that felt wonderful! I've wanted to say that ever since I met you, young man," she exclaimed to Mark. "Do you really think now, in this situation, that type of petty bullying is helpful? No, don't answer. Just stand there with your trap shut and let me tell you something. What Dara said is the exact truth of the situation. You would not know that nor understand as you mainly read comic books. So....Hush!"

It was very difficult for Alex not to burst out with laughter at the expression on Mark's face. With his red hair and fair skin, he looked like a tomato that was about to burst. Mason finally stepped in and gave his buddy a jab in the ribs with his elbow and a quick shake of his head. Mark took a step back and kept his eyes on the ground as he tried to cool down.

"Now as I was saying, we should leave here as soon as possible. I would not bother going back to the hotel as it is in the wrong direction and we have the important things such as money and passports with us. Clothing can be replaced. Time cannot. We should walk northeast until we find a sporting goods store and then buy backpacks, camping supplies and bikes if we can. Money should be working for a few more hours before people start to understand the situation. Some form of weapon should also be procured. Things will get very dangerous and it's best to be prepared to defend oneself." Mrs. Moore stated in a no-nonsense way.

Alex couldn't help but be a bit shocked by Mrs. Moore. She had always been a very matronly lady and somewhat strict but this was a not at all what Alex would have expected to lie at the core of her personality. She had always enjoyed Mrs. Moore's classes as they tended to be a challenge with some good debates, but this was an altogether different lady.

"Mrs. Moore," Mason stepped forward. "Why would we try to cross two countries overland when we are so close to the ocean? We could find a boat and easily sail all the way back up to Canada. It would be much quicker and not so physically demanding."

Before Mrs. Moore could reply, Mrs. Davis and Mrs. Hardsky the parent chaperones, along with a man no one knew came up to the group. Mrs. Davis started up right away.

"Norma, this gentleman is also Canadian and he has advised us that our best option is to go to the Canadian Embassy here. They are required to care for us and see to it that we get home," she said triumphantly.

Mrs. Moore looked the man over and questioned him. "Where are you from sir?"

"Please call me Paul. I'm here with my wife and daughter from Toronto."

Mrs. Moore then started firing questions at the man. "The Embassy, is it not in downtown Los Angeles? Wouldn't you have to walk through a lot of very poor, possibly dangerous, neighbourhoods? Other than allowing us inside, what do you think the Embassy could do for us? Won't there be thousands of Canadians going there? With no transportation how will they send us home? And if they can't send us home, how will they feed us? Thank you, Mr. Paul but I do not believe that you can answer any of those questions with the answers that would make it worth going there."

As she started to turn away from him, he grabbed her arm and with panic in his voice loudly stated, "It is their job! They have to take care of us!"

Mrs. Moore gave the man a very steely glare. "Unhand me and remove yourself from this area, sir. Attend to your own family and I will attend to my students."

The man moved away angrily and Mrs. Davis immediately took up his case. "Norma really, that is the best idea. We can't be responsible for all these students in a crisis! We need to go to the authorities for help and the Canadian Embassy is our best bet."

Mrs. Moore sadly shook her head and looked around at all the student in the class. Everyone seemed to have been listening to all the discussions about what to do. Most students looked unsure and confused and some were still crying. The only other teacher, Ms. Scott, was still sobbing in the arms of another parent.

Mrs. Moore stepped away from Mrs. Davis and raised her arms. "Alright students, your attention, please! We have been discussing the best way to go forward and there are two different opinions of the best course forward. We will discuss both with you and answer any questions to the best of our ability and then you will vote on what you feel is the best choice for each of you."

Mrs. Davis was incensed by this and turned to Mrs. Moore with, "You can't be serious! They are children and don't know what's best for them! Letting them vote is ridiculous and totally irresponsible!" she said in a huff.

"I disagree." Mrs. Moore cut her off. "They are all sixteen and older and after being informed, have the right to choose. After all, this decision may mean life or death for them and I am confident that they are mature enough to have a say in their future."

"Well, MY daughter will not be voting anything! This is a decision for adults, not children," she said forcefully.

"Very well, Mrs. Davis as you are her parent that is between the two of you. But as the rest of the young adults are without parental representation they will make their own decisions."

She turned back to the students and noticed that a few were smiling and that Mrs. Davis's daughter was looking miserable.

"As I was saying, the first choice is that we will all try to walk to the Canadian Embassy in Los Angeles which is about 20 to 30 miles away. We will then hope that they will help us to get home." she paused looking at everyone's faces to be sure they all understood the scenario and then continued. "The other choice is to try to leave the city as quickly as possible and hope to find bikes or other transportation along the way. After leaving the city we would then continue our way north towards Canada.

Now, you have all heard the different discussions about both these options and I will try to answer any questions." she finished and waited expectantly.

Alex and the other students around her looked to each other and Quinn said, "Let's step away for a minute." They all moved away from their teacher and once again it was Quinn that started the discussion. "Does anyone here want to go to the Embassy?" he asked. Everyone shook their heads no and Mason and Mark made comments like "idiots" and "suicide".

"All right so we are all agreed that we need to get out of here and on the road." He quickly did a head count. "Ok there are ten of us to start and who knows how many others will want to join us. But if it's ten plus Mrs. Moore I think that would make a good team to work out duties like standing watch and camp chores. And we can rotate so no one has all the crap work." Quinn was about to continue when Mason jumped in. "Hey, who made you team captain? I'm the quarterback here and I don't agree with your plan at all and neither do my friends!"

Then everyone started talking at once and the group quickly split into two camps. Josh and Mark were starting a shoving contest when Emily yelled out, "STOP IT!"

It was such a surprise that everyone stopped talking and pushing and turned to stare at her. "Mason, Quinn we have to work together on this or no one will survive! Mason if you don't like Quinn's plan then tell us what you think we should do and we can discuss it. But no more fighting! The longer it takes for us to figure it out, the harder it will be once we get out there." then she sat down on the ground and waited. Mason looked like he wasn't too happy his girlfriend had called him out but took a deep breath and sat down beside her.

Once everyone was sitting again and looking to him he began. "Ok, I agree we need to get out of here but I think going thousands of miles across two countries is stupid. I say we head to the coast and get a boat. We sail it right up to Vancouver and then hike the rest of the way home." he said with a smug smile.

Quinn was looking at him waiting for more. When he realized that was it, he shook his head and said, "That's it? Go get a boat and sail it away? Haven't you been listening? Nothing works! Boats have motors same as cars. Even if you found an old one, what would you do? Steal it? We are going to try to buy bikes. Not steal them. Ok, so now you have stolen a boat. Do you have any idea on how to sail on the ocean? Man, come on! At least on land, you can't drown and what about food and water? That's almost as bad as staying put and waiting for help!"

Mason gave him a look of contempt and told him, "I'm not a total idiot you know! I was thinking of getting a sailboat so it's just a matter of getting out of the marina and then using the sails. As for stealing it, well it's a brand new world and survival of the fittest is the new law of the land. We can stock up on food and water on the way to the coast and we can also fish if we have too. It beats killing ourselves walking or biking thousands of miles. My old man always says "Work smarter, not harder." Anyways that's what we are doing and I don't need to talk about it with you. If you make it home I'll be sure to have a cold beer waiting for you. You will really need it by then."

Before Quinn could say anything else Mrs. Moore called them back over to the main group.

Once they were sitting again she began, "Now that we have answered your questions it's time to vote. All those wanting to head to the Embassy raise your hands." Alex was shocked that all the students and adults except for Mrs. Moore and her and Mason's group raised their hands. With a frown of disappointment on her face, Mrs. Moore said, "And those wanting to leave the city?" The ten students with Alex and Mrs. Moore all raised their hands. That was it, eleven people to leave out of the whole class. With a resigned sigh Mrs. Moore continued, "Although I disagree with your decision, it is yours to make. Mrs. Davis will now take over and you may follow her directions. You ten students who are leaving follow me to the side." As Mrs. Moore started walking away from the main group,

Mrs. Davis realized what that meant and immediately started objecting. "What are you doing? You can't leave! You children join the main group right this minute. You lost the vote so you will be coming to the Embassy!"

Mrs. Moore rounded on her forcefully and told her "Shut up! You are not their parent. They have made their decision and as the adult responsible for them I give it my blessing. I will know that at least some of my students will survive this. Now go back and prepare the rest to get moving." she finished while turning her back on Mrs. Davis in dismissal.

"Norma you can't talk to me that way! And what about the rest of the children? They are your responsibility as well." she said in desperation. The thought of being responsible for all the students erased the smugness of getting her own way.

With a look of exhaustion Mrs. Moore turned back and wearily said, "Mrs. Davis, I will be accompanying you and the rest of the students to the Embassy."

"But you don't want to go there. I don't understand you at all!" she said in exasperation.

"All the students are in my charge. And even though I strongly disagree with your choice, someone has to try and keep you alive and that seems to be me. Now please go back and get everyone ready to go while I talk to this group."

With a look of disbelief on her face, Mrs. Davis walked away.

"Well if we do make it home, I'm sure that one will have plenty to say to the school board! And I for one would welcome that if it is the worst outcome of this tragedy. Now we must make haste as time is slipping away! Have you all decided what to do?" Mrs. Moore looked to the group expectantly.

Alex couldn't believe what was happening. "Why aren't they listening Mrs. Moore? This is crazy. Please come with us!"

Mrs. Moore turned to Alex with a sad smile and said, "Alex I'm sorry, I can't go with you. Most people are sheep. They can't think for themselves. They will only follow and look to others to take care of them. You students are all leaders and I know that you will do fine without me. The rest will need to be taken care of and I believe it will be up to me to do that." She turned back to the group, "What have you decided?"

Mason began by explaining to Mrs. Moore his sailing ideas and Quinn explained his.

"Alright, both are sound ideas. Are you sure that you won't stay together?"

At the boys and their friend's negative answers, she said, "I am positive that you would do better if you stayed together but there is also a better chance of at least one group making it. So that's that. Mason, there is not a lot of advice I can give you about sailing but I will say this. Work together as a team. Stay vigilant for danger and don't give trust easily to strangers. The best judge will be your intuition. Also be reminded that even though this is a new lawless land you are setting out in, you will have to live with the decisions that you make along the way. Help others when you can but always keep your group's safety as a priority. Good luck to you and may God watch over you." With that, she gave him a pat on the back and nods to Lisa and Mark.

She turned to Quinn and said, "I don't know which group will have the hardest journey so all I have said applies to you as well. Your journey will be more physically demanding, so rest when you feel safe but don't waste time. The longer this goes on the worse conditions will get and the worse people will behave. Remember that it is a different world out there and some rules will have to change. If you feel threatened do not hesitate to take action and if you are truly in a situation where it is your life against someone else, act accordingly. Do not let that burden you deeply as you are not only saving your own life but probably others in the future. Do you understand what I am saying?" She looked around and met all of our eyes.

Alex spoke up clearly, "If someone is trying to kill or hurt us, we should defend ourselves and if it means that person dies we shouldn't fall apart over it. Is that what you mean?"

"Yes" was all Mrs. Moore said.

"Alright Mason, you, Lisa and Mark should go now. Stop at the closest convenience store and get a map and some water. The sooner the better, it's going to get crazy out in the city soon." Mrs. Moore stood to see them off.

"Emily is coming too," Mason announced.

Alex's immediate response was, "No she is not!" and turned to face Emily who was looking down quietly crying.

"Emily?" Alex asked. "What's he talking about? You can't go with them! You can't leave me." Alex cried.

Emily looked up and met her best friend's eyes, "I'm sorry Lex. I'm going with Mason."

Start a new adventure with Land A Stranded Novel FREE at all e-book retailers!

Also By Theresa Shaver

The Stranded Series

Land – A Stranded Novel

Alex, Quinn, Josh, Cooper and Dara - setting out on foot with nothing more than some soon to be worthless cash and a little advice from a trusted teacher, they walk through a burning city that has come to a halt. The devastation they see as they make their way out of the city is a small part of the horror that the nation will become. As the days go by with no food deliveries and no water flowing from taps, civilization will start to crumble and it will be survival of the fittest. With five States and half a Province to cross they will need to plan well, count on each other and pray for a little luck. Even with that, chances are slim of getting home when you are Stranded.

Sea – A Stranded Novel

Emily and her friends head to the California coast to find a boat back to Canada. They all felt that it would be much easier and quicker to sail home rather than go over land. They were wrong. Not only will they have to fight their way through the lawless city and the terrifying ocean, they will have a journey of hardship and loss as the biggest threat will come from within their own group. The trip home will change them all for good and bad as they are stranded at SEA.

Home - A Stranded Novel

Five went by Land and five went by Sea. Nine made it through the chaos Home. With their town under siege, and their families both prisoners and slaves, they will have the biggest challenge yet. After witnessing the pain and suffering in the town, the group of teens has to decide just how far they are willing to go to save them. Life sucks when you are Home, but still Stranded.

City Escape – A Stranded Novel

Mrs. Moore and the rest of the students that remained in California face the harsh reality that no one is coming to help them. As the city burns around them, they are surrounded by 18 million people with one goal…survival. Will Mrs. Moore's determination be enough to save them? Surrounded by chaos, they must work together to find a shelter before it's too late.

Frozen – A Stranded Novel

When the teen's town is hit with a devastating virus, they take it upon themselves to travel first to the closest military encampment to find the medicine their loved ones so desperately need. Stonewalled at every turn they make the hard decision to embark on an epic journey to a faraway city to search the ruins for help they need.

Traveling through a Frozen wasteland, they not only have to fight the elements and other survivors but also the inner struggles and changes each one has to accept and live with.
It's not just the weather that has Frozen.

The Endless Winter Series

Snow and Ash – An Endless Winter Novel

Bomb after bomb dropped across the globe sending the world into a seemingly never-ending nuclear winter.
Skylar Ross is ten that day when she's ripped from dance classes and sleepovers to being an orphan in a prepper's paradise of a mountain bunker. Her determination to protect her baby brother keeps her locked away with nothing but responsibility and loneliness. Her father's words are a continuous echo, "Trust no one. Help no one."
Rex Larson is eleven that day. He's left stranded on the side of the road in a strange place far from home when his mother dies that first day. With his own small brother to look after, he is lost and alone. Rex has no choice but to trust complete strangers with his and his brother's future.

Two different survivors in two different circumstances spend the next seven years trying to survive until an explosive meeting changes both their courses and lives forever. Trust is almost impossible when you spend your whole life in the SNOW & ASH.

Rain and Ruin – An Endless Winter Novel

A hailstorm of bombs has blasted the world into a nuclear winter. The survivors have now spent seven long years in the snow and ash scratching out a lonely, hard existence.

Although comfortable in her safe and supplied bunker, Skylar Ross longed for more of a life than what she has. She thought she found it when she rescued Rex but the evil that followed him inside her home threatened the one person she holds most dear. Can she put aside her mistrust of others and give him and his people a second chance?

Rex Larson fell hard for Skylar and was excited about his group joining her in the safety of her bunker until he was betrayed by one of his own. Exiled back out into the cold, he prays that Skylar will change her mind.

Forced to flee the town when a deadly gang moves in, the survivors huddle in the cold hoping the gang won't find them and for Skylar to change her mind. When the weather turns for the first time in seven years, they don't know if it means the earth is starting to heal or if it's just more ruin.

http://www.theresashaver.com/books

Made in the USA
Middletown, DE
11 July 2018